SEE ME THROUGH

Ginger Lee

Copyright 2017 by Ginger Lee

Cover photo by Kaspars Grinvalds

Chapter One

Seth browsed the photography section of The Book Bank without paying attention to the actual books. He'd pick one up, flip through the pages, and place it back on the shelf. He did this multiple times, attempting to ease closer to the girl standing at the display in the front of the store without looking like a creep.

In Seth's line of work, he made a mental note of every detail. He took pleasure in studying his subject before snapping a picture. She looked to be about five foot six. She wore a white T-shirt with a blue scarf. With her honey-colored hair pulled back in a ponytail, her heart-shaped face and lovely round cheekbones were on full display. And that mouth—that oh-so-feminine—parted mouth complete with a full bottom lip that got his heart racing. He'd love to catch a glimpse of her eyes, to see if they were a baby blue or maybe even a light shade of green similar to his own, but a book on conceptual art, kept her engaged, so he couldn't get a good look. He scanned her body; observing long slender fingers cradling the book down to her lean, athletic build and ample curves.

She was a rare natural beauty, Seth noted to himself. If she would only glance up from the page, he would make a move to introduce himself. But it didn't seem as though that would happen today, and Seth needed to get back to the office, so he walked out of the bookstore. He paused to glance at her through the window one more time, unable to ignore the nagging voice in his head telling him to go back in and seize the day.

When the girl finally looked up, Seth straightened in surprise and lifted his hand to wave, when he heard a commotion to his right. He turned his head and saw a man masked in a black balaclava, pointing a gun at a small, older whimpering woman. He had already stripped her purse off her shoulder and was now demanding her jewelry.

"Hurry up or else!" Her attacker demanded in a deep scratchy voice as the frail woman slipped off her cheap looking bracelets which he stuffed in his dirty jean pocket, but she struggled removing her wedding band. She gave it one more swift tug and the ring flew to the ground. In frustration, he panicked and cocked the hammer back on the silver revolver.

Hearing the unmistakable click, Seth lunged forward, grabbed the woman in a bear hug, and turned to put himself between the gunman and the woman just as the man fired. Seth clutched his right side and dropped to his knees. He clenched his teeth, hoping that would distract his mind from the intense pain. His ears rang as he watched the mugger take off down the adjacent ally.

Rae watched the scene unfold through the window of the book store. After shaking away her disbelief, she jerked her phone out of her pocket and called 911 from inside the store. By the time she ran outside, the shooter was gone, but the smell of gunpowder still hung in the air.

Some had scattered at the shot. Others were standing around unsure of what to do. Things like this never happened on this area of the city. The gray-haired woman was crying over the handsome man lying on the sidewalk, bleeding from the right side of his grey tee. He didn't make a noise. His eyes were fixated on the sky above. Rae tore the blue scarf from her neck and held it over the wound, ignoring his wince as he glanced at her. She felt his eyes on her for only a moment before they rolled upwards, as his lids closed. Rae was pretty sure he passed out, but she could feel an adequate pulse. It only took a few minutes for the ambulance to arrive, and EMS took over the scene.

The police took statements from witnesses inside The Big Brew, the coffee shop next to The Book Bank. Rae owned the shop and lived upstairs in a one-room apartment. After giving her account, she instructed her employees Sarah and Quincy to get the police anything they needed, then ran upstairs to shower. She had the stranger's blood on her arms and clothes. Rae placed the clothes in a trash bag, and felt something in the pocket of her jeans. It was the woman's wedding ring. She didn't even remember picking it up. She was full of nervous energy, replaying the event in her mind. Her thoughts were unnerving as she played out scenarios of the beautiful man not making it, or being in great pain. Rae truly believed the old saying about things happening for a reason. She felt strongly about her own energy in the universe, and wished good vibes his way.

Seth woke up a couple of hours later in a hospital bed. The walls were a sterile beige and the room smelled of Lysol, but the bed itself was comfortable enough. A dry erase board on the wall directly across from the bed read, "UMC Brackenridge, Nurse on Duty Julie Renner, RN."

Because it all happened so fast, he couldn't remember the exact details. The mugger had concealed his identity with a mask, so that wasn't going to help the police. They probably wouldn't ever find the guy.

Seth did remember waving to the lovely girl in the bookstore. She had blushed and smirked at him through the glass right before the trouble ensued behind him. He remembered seeing white clouds floating through the turquoise blue heavens and the beautiful girl from the store by his side. He recalled the determined look in her green eyes when she jerked the scarf from her neck and shoved it to his side. She wasn't scared. After that, his mind went blank.

The door to his room opened, and who he assumed was Nurse Julie waltzed in. She had a sly smile on her red lips, and she knew how to walk to get a man's attention. Though he still felt groggy, he noticed her red nails as she rubbed his arm and slowly injected more pain medication into his IV.

"Rest up handsome," she said as his eyes fluttered shut and he drifted back to sleep.

Rae had trouble sleeping that night. She had never witnessed a shooting before. She tossed. She turned. She wasn't afraid of the mugger, or that it happened so close to her shop. To be involved in a traumatic experience with Tall and Handsome, watch him be taken away to the hospital, and never hear a word on his status twisted her nerves into frayed shreds. She wished she knew if he was okay. She grabbed her cell phone multiple times, throwing it back down on the pillow beside her, deciding not to call the hospital. What would she say? Who would she ask for? She wasn't even sure which facility he was taken to. Eventually she succumbed to sleep.

The next morning it was back to business, and Rae surprisingly slept like a baby. She knew the cops who came to The Big Brew to investigate the crime. She also knew that muscled-up officer Sam Preston would likely be back in soon for his daily black coffee. Sam had been overly fond of her since college. He didn't show much interest in classes or studying, but always showed up at the library when she was there. He even resorted to dating Jules, one of her friends, when Rae hadn't shown any interest.

Not that Sam wasn't attractive. He spent more time at the gym than in class. His jet black hair and blue eyes made him popular with the sorority girls. His stint in college didn't last long, and he went to work for the Austin PD. It suited him. He still flirted with Rae endlessly, and came to The Big Brew almost every morning before his shift started. She had never been too friendly or given him any hope of dating her. Rae had only been concerned with creating and maintaining a successful business. She graduated from the McCombs School of Business at the University of

Texas. Her favorite alternative classes were in art, but her dream was to own a cozy coffee shop.

She pulled on brown corduroys and a gray Dreamers T-shirt, then threw a navy cardigan over that. Before heading downstairs to get the morning started, she put the wedding ring in a Ziploc to give to Sam. Business always picked up in late September when the Austin City Limits music festival was in full swing.

Sam shifted his weight from left foot to right while outside the door in his dark navy uniform.

"You're at it early this morning," she said after unlocking the door and allowing him to step inside.

He grabbed her hand immediately. "How are you? I wanted to come back by to check on you, but things got hectic at the station."

She pulled her hand away to flip over the old fashioned Open sign. He put his long arm around her shoulder as she was trying to put some space in between them. His cologne was too strong. It was always overwhelming.

"I'm fine," she told him. He walked her back to the counter, and she ducked out from under his heavy arm. She tied on a red apron and started the coffee machines. Rae opened every weekday morning.

She set a mug of black coffee in front of Sam, before turning to start the sweet tea for the guests who would be in for lunch. Rae could always count on several repeat customers who worked in the area. She could sense the officer's eyes investigating her backside. Over her shoulder she said, "I'm not afraid. It was a guy grabbing a purse. It's not like he was robbing my place. I'm sure he was on some kind of drugs."

"But he shot a man," he replied.

That reminded her of the old woman's ring. "Here." She pulled the bag from her pocket and sat it on the counter. "Can you give this back to her?"

As if on cue, Sarah, Rae's best employee, walked in, interrupting the conversation she didn't want to continue. Sarah thrived in her business courses in college and was an excellent manager. She was young and beautiful with tanned skin and onyx hair that fell down to her waist.

Rae attempted on several occasions to set her up with Sam, but he would say he only had eyes for her. Rae would roll her eyes and laugh it off.

As Sarah passed, she patted Sam on the knee and went straight to the stereo to turn on some alternative music.

Rae asked Sam, "How is the guy?"

Sam downed the coffee and stood up, "He'll make it. He did get a collapsed lung, but the bullet went straight through, and amazingly didn't hit the lady. I'll be back around later. Call me if you need me Rae."

"Will do," she replied.

After he was gone, Sarah sang, "You have a stalker."

Rae gave her a glaring look as customers began to filter in.

Chapter Two

Seth woke at 9 a.m. Sunshine streamed through the hospital window. The ticking of the generic black and white clock was the only noise he heard. He immediately noticed the chest tube was gone and had been replaced with thick bandages and a flesh colored ace wrap. His IV was missing. A blood pressure cuff was the only tether left in place. Nurse Julie didn't come into the room until ten.

He was anxious to leave the hospital and get back to his laptop. A little over a month ago, he'd relocated to Austin from St. George, Utah, a place he grew up and loved. His family was there, but he had landed a promotion in advertising that transferred him to Texas. Seth was a talented photographer, and his market was the outdoors. He could make any hiking trail, river, mountain or campground look like a dream destination. He was far from the outdoors at the moment.

When Julie came in, he let her know he wanted to leave as soon as possible.

She looked disappointed and said, "Aren't you going to miss me?"

"Of course," he answered. "You get the best nurse award, but I have work to do and I need a shower."

She smiled and said, "Doc is planning on discharging you today. You'll go home with pain meds and my phone number in case you need anything."

When she sat down on the edge of his bed, it made him uncomfortable. He sat up and swung his legs over the opposite side to get away. Julie must have realized she wasn't getting anywhere, because she stood and moved toward the door.

"I'll be getting my things together and waiting for the okay from Dr. Davidson," he told her over his shoulder.

As soon as she left, the door opened again and Dr. Davidson walked in. "I hear you're ready to leave our fine establishment." He chuckled as he extended his hand toward Seth. "Take care of yourself. Call us if you have any questions, and try not to be a hero, if you can help it."

Seth replied, "I can't thank you enough, doctor. I will take it easy for a few days, I promise."

Seth reluctantly let a cute blonde candy striper push him out in a wheelchair, and she took her time getting to the entrance of the hospital. He was very sore, and he had forgotten that an ambulance had brought him here. He gingerly sat on a bench in front of the building and called a cab.

Saturday. How was it already Saturday?

Seth was usually up with the sun, but not today. It had been a tough three days on his own, but the perks of being basically immobile with his laptop meant he had gotten a lot of research done on the local parks and hiking trails. He needed to get out of the apartment, yet wasn't quite ready to tackle a full day in the great outdoors. Lady Bird Lake would be on the calendar for tomorrow.

Seth had been surviving off luke-warm food delivery and hadn't had a decent cup of coffee in days. He knew The Big Brew was right beside the bookstore. He had thought about the girl in The Book Bank every day. Hell, he had dreamed about her every night. He saw her face looking down, not into his eyes, but at the bloody scarf she held to his side. His angel. He was itching to see if, by chance, she would be around town.

It was a busy Saturday and things seemed to be back to normal as far as Rae could tell. It had been four days with no reportable crime on the block. Thankfully, the shooting incident had not deterred customers. On the contrary, the shop buzzed with caffeine lovers.

Rae would never complain about all the business, but a quick glance at the clock told her it was after two in the afternoon, and she desperately wanted to run next door to pick up the book she ordered last week.

Of course, instead of going straight to the counter, Rae got sucked into the art section of the store. It was right up front, so she couldn't resist. Art, in any form, calmed her. She had not painted since college, but dreamed of having walls full of art someday. Rae felt the warm presence of someone coming up behind her, peering over her shoulder. She could smell the cologne, and she swore she heard him sniff her hair.

"See anything interesting?" she asked in a cool tone.

Sam Preston's voice replied, "Not any books but…"

She stiffened. "You know, you could actually try reading one, or at least looking at the pictures." She closed the Salvador Dali book with a hard snap. This attribute of Sam's turned her off. He had never appreciated culture. As she headed to the cashier to get the Vladimir Kush book she ordered, she decided to purchase the Dali book as well.

A tall, dark haired, exceptionally handsome man walked in the door, and the clerk jumped excitedly from behind the counter, leaving Rae with the money still in her hand.

Laura Lee, the clerk, hugged Adonis' arm and practically squealed, "Honey! How have you been? We've been worried sick about our brave hero!"

Rae realized then who he was. She felt a pull in her stomach and got nervous for no reason. She immediately wished she had dressed better this morning. She wondered if she had coffee breath, and if she had used hand lotion after washing up the morning mugs.

Laura Lee boldly asked to see his scar, and he reluctantly pulled up the edge of his grey Henley. There, on his right side, was the exit wound with two black stitches still in place. Rae assumed he also had one on the back where the bullet entered. There was still major greenish yellow bruising visible.

Laura Lee's shrill voice snapped Rae back to the here and now.

"Rae!" She squealed with excitement, and pulled Seth along to present him to Rae. "Here's your hero, Mr. Reagan! Rae Bennett. She's the one who stayed with you and kept you from bleedin' to death 'til the ambulance came."

In a deep, silky voice he said, "Seth. It's Seth Reagan. I've been thinking about you. I mean, I really wanted to thank you for everything."

Rae felt her cheeks getting hot and reddening, looking up at his perfect features. "Thank you for saving that woman," she managed to say. "I'm so happy to get to meet you, not lying on the sidewalk. I'm just glad I was able to help in some way."

She had forgotten about Sam, but remembered when he put his arm around her shoulders.

"Mr. Reagan, good to see you on your feet." Sam puffed out his chest, trying hard to be the alpha male.

Seth took a step back and replied, "Yes, me too. Thank you, officer, I'm getting there."

Sam added, "I didn't know my Rae Rae had it in her, but she held her own." Hearing the words "Rae Rae" made her cringe. She knew Seth heard them as well.

Thankfully, the universe saved the day when Sam's phone rang. It was a call he couldn't ignore. "See you later," he told Rae.

She didn't even acknowledge him. She wished Sam had kept his hands to himself in front of Seth, but Sam had always been a little too handsy.

Laura Lee insisted, "Mr. Reagan, you have to try Rae's coffee! It's the best in town."

Seth returned next to Rae and smiled. "Oh really? The Big Brew is yours?"

She answered, "Um, yeah. For four years now. I want you to come have a cup on the house. Owner's special. But, I really need to pay for these books, Laura Lee."

The clerk ran back around to ring up the sale.

Rae turned to Seth again, "Are you busy now?"

His lips curved into a smile, "Nope. I'd love to see the place."

As they walked the ten steps it took to reach her shop, Rae notice that Seth had to be at least 6'2, and smelled of Irish Spring. She hadn't been this excited about a guy since high school, when she'd had a silly little crush on the out-of-her-league captain of the football team. She tried to tame her feelings. She had only just met the man for goodness sake. She couldn't deny the instant attraction the moment they looked into each other's green eyes in the bookstore.

Seth held open the door and smelled fresh coffee beans brewing. The shop was bigger than he'd imagined with brick floors and walls. A worn, green velvet sofa sat in front facing the large shop window.

Intimate booths lined the wall on the right, while café tables sat beside a wooden stage on the left. A long wooden service counter in the very back held the cash register.

Salvador Dali prints and various thrift store landscape oil paintings decorated the walls. A string of clear lights hung over the stage flanked by scarlet red velvet curtains. It was quite charming. It smelled like fresh coffee bean heaven, and he was on cloud nine after meeting the angel who saved him. His angel. What a story they could tell their children.

Woah, he thought. He needed to get control of himself. His near future hadn't included any of this. His siblings were married with children. He loved being Uncle Seth, but a father? A husband? His career had kept him entertained and fulfilled since college.

He had landed his first photography job weeks before graduation. Before moving to Austin, he'd dated Claire, his sister's best friend, for five years. He knew it had only continued so long because it was easy. As soon as he made the decision to take the job in another state, he ended it. Seth was very focused on his job and thrilled for a change of scenery.

And he couldn't deny the excitement at the thought of meeting someone else, like a new adventure.

He couldn't help the carnal need to know Rae more. She helped save his life, and he wanted to protect her. But what about the cop? His gaze dropped to her hand. No ring on her finger. Charged by a glimmer of hope, Seth followed her toward the counter at the rear of the shop.

Rae patted a high, leather stool, and Seth slid onto the seat next to her.

"It's pretty busy in here." Seth looked around the room. "Glad to see a robbery attempt didn't scare customers away."

"Right? And it's just after three. We don't usually get this busy until after dinner."

"You should set one up every few months. I'll save someone, you save me. Ongoing marketing gimmick."

Rae laughed, confirming Seth's opinion that she was an angel. He'd never heard a sweeter sound than her genuine laugh.

Still smiling, she asked the girl across the counter for two mugs of coffee. "Sarah, this is Seth Reagan. You know, the bravest guy I think I've ever met, who took a bullet for a perfect stranger. We actually just ran into each other next door."

Sarah's face lit up with delight. "Oh! I can't believe you are here! We've been wondering about you every day. You look great, considering."

A husky, college-aged kid with curly brown hair tied into a pony tail came up with his arms raised and theatrically said, "He's alive!"

Rae laughed and joked, "That's Quincy, my bouncer."

Seth let out a deep laugh and said, "Thanks! It's great to meet both of you. I've only been in town a few weeks, and after what happened, I was afraid I wouldn't meet one person in Austin besides hospital staff."

"What a welcome," Sarah said before shuffling away to help another guest.

Seth laughed again, unable to keep his grin from Rae, the girl who put the smile on his face.

Conversation with her was easy. It didn't take long for Seth to spill his life story. They talked about everything; from his photography, to growing up in Utah, art and coffee. He told her about his sister, brother, nieces and nephews.

"Wow," Rae remarked. "I absolutely love that you are so close with your family. I can't even relate. My parents divorced shortly after I was born. I never met my father, and my mother never remarried. I'm an only child."

"Are you and your mother close?" he asked concerned.

"Well, we were when I was younger. My mom smoked her entire life. She got pretty sick when I was five, and two years later she passed away from severe lung disease. My grandmother, Pearl, made everything okay though. She moved in when mom got sick. I was always her number one priority. She actually passed away two years ago."

Rae hadn't shared her life with many people, but Seth made it easy. It was like the universe forged a quick connection with this beautiful man she barely knew. She didn't want to come off as too eager, but she was having the best time getting to know Seth in her little coffee shop.

He was moved to hear her story. He was amazed that she was able to overcome the obstacles in her life and succeed in accomplishing her goals.

Although he had already gotten a pretty good idea of Sam's character, he inquired more about Super Cop. "So…officer Preston. Is he? Are you?"

"Are you asking if I'm single?" she said smiling. "I've never dated Sam, and never will. And, yes, I'm single, if that's what you were asking."

"Good to know. Yes. Yeah, me too. Just so you know," he said with a wink, which made Rae flutter inside.

Neither wanted the night to end, but it was now dark outside. They hadn't noticed the customers had all gone, and Sarah and Quincy had already ended their shifts.

Seth stretched his long arms over his head and asked, "So, will you be here in the morning?"

"Well, I actually live upstairs, but Sarah and Quincy work Sundays for me. I have the whole day off," she replied.

"Would it be crazy to ask you to come to the river with me tomorrow? I have some work to do there and you may not be the least bit interested, but…"

Rae interrupted, "Yes. I mean, I'm up for it."

His eyes lit up, "Great! And I'll take it easy on you. I'm still recovering," he joked as he patted his side.

"Oh, playing the sympathy card, huh?" Rae laughed sweetly.

Seth stood up and offered his hand, which Rae took with no hesitation. He pulled her to her feet and didn't let go until they reached the front door.

"Meet you right here at nine a.m. sharp," he stated.

"I'll be here with hiking boots on," she said with a click of her heels.

They were alone, but he didn't try to kiss her. He wanted to badly, but instead gave her a hug on his left, less painful, side. Then, he stepped out onto the sidewalk and watched her lock up from the inside. He stayed until he saw her disappear up the steps. This was the second time he had watched her through a window.

Chapter Three

Rae would be lying to herself to say she wasn't a little disappointed. She had never wanted to taste a man's lips as much as she did at the moment, but was relieved at the same time. She would be insane to kiss the man on the first day she met him and didn't want to look desperate for crying out loud. She had a feeling it would happen soon enough.

Instead of dwell on it, she picked out her hiking clothes since she was too excited to go straight to bed. As she laid clothes on the plush purple velvet chair in her bedroom, she tried to recall every detail of the evening with Seth. She marveled at how tall he was, and how she'd fit so perfectly in his arms. Feeling silly at the thought, she held her t-shirt to her lips. Yet her mind wandered to how badly she'd wanted to touch his long fingers again. She had noticed them repeatedly while Seth sipped his coffee, scratched his chin, or tapped them on the table while they talked. She bet he really looked sexy holding his camera.

She tossed and turned all night until the alarm went off at eight. She showered with her favorite peppermint scrub to wake herself up. Rae hadn't picked out her outfit the night before for a date since she was in high school and was ready in record time. She could hear Sarah and Quincy singing along with Radiohead downstairs. She was smiling when she skipped down the steps.

Seth walked in right on time wearing a big grin on his face, camera in hand. Rae had been right about how he looked. His large hands made the camera look small. He was beyond sexy in his cargo shorts and white tee that showed every muscle in his chest and back. He snapped a few shots of The Big Brew and said, "I hope you don't mind. I would love to include your place as a pre-trailblazing stop for bagels and coffee."

Rae felt honored and knew that would be a huge spur for business. "Are you serious? Because that would be wonderful!"

He grinned, obviously pleased by her approval of his idea. "Well, it *is* the best around."

Her stomach did a flip, hearing his genuine appreciation. "It's the only one you've been to in Austin," she said.

He replied in a sultry tone, "You know I'm partial."

Rae felt heat in her cheeks again. Seth must've noticed, because he pulled her into a warm, strong embrace. He flipped the camera around and leaned down cheek to cheek to get a shot of them together.

While they were still close, she felt his breath on her ear as he whispered, "You smell delicious. Like a candy cane." Rae almost melted like chocolate right then and there.

Seth seemed a bit reluctant to remove his hand from where it rested on her waist and she imagined it traveling to other locations. She knew her green worn out tee felt like silk, but she hoped his hesitation had a deeper meaning.

"Thanks for holding down the fort!" She called to Sarah and Quincy.

"Great to see you both again!" Seth lifted his camera, as if waving, before tucking it into his backpack. Then he tugged Rae out the door.

As they began walking, he laced their fingers together and asked, "Is this ok?"

"Yes, it's nice," she replied feeling the heat rise in her cheeks again. His warm, firm grasp had her heart racing. As they neared the middle of the trail, Seth took out his camera and went to work.

Rae was content to watch him in his element. His body moved with such fluidity while he worked. Desire bloomed, and she wondered what kind of lover he would be. His height, good looks, sexy voice and the way he carried himself made him the perfect specimen. Seth Reagan was the total package, and when he held her hand, she wished he was hers and hers alone.

The park attracted lots of tourists and locals with the sunny, breezy weather. There were bikers and hikers along the urban path. Kayaks and canoes slipped across the Colorado River. This place was unlike any of his previous locations in the mountains and canyons of Utah. He got a perfect shot of Rae next to the water with soaring skyscrapers as the backdrop.

She made the perfect subject. Her green eyes were like kryptonite. Her athletic build was exactly his type, but what he admired her for the most was her independence and self-confidence. She wasn't confident per say, in her looks, but rather her ability to make something of herself. She had done just that. She knew what she wanted and went for it. Seth hoped to place himself in her sight. He wanted her for his own. After knowing Rae a few short days, he knew he never wanted to let her go.

They sat close to one another on a bench in a cool, shaded area. Rae began scrolling through the shots he had taken on his camera, commenting how gorgeous they were, even before any editing. Seth took out a big notebook and began writing. He wrote about hiking, biking, running and the quiet, serene spots as well.

Rae knew the food trucks were not too much farther down the path. She stood up to stretch her legs. "You stay here and let your creative juices flow. I'll be back in ten," she said.

He put his pen down, "I'm sorry! Are you bored? I wasn't even thinking."

Rae shook her head. "No! I'm not bored. To tell you the truth, I'm hungry."

He laughed, "Me too. Let me buy us some lunch."

She started walking, and replied, "Nope. I know where the soft pretzels are." She blew him a kiss and went on her way.

Rae smelled earthy hops, smoked sausage, and cinnamon churros before she arrived at the square. She got in line for the big soft pretzels. The tall brunette in front of her glanced over her shoulder and lit up with recognition. It was Jules, Miss Perfect from college.

She began to speak so quickly, Rae could only blink back at her.

"Rae Bennett! You been doin' ok? I've been meaning to stop by your little shop, but just haven't made it in. A nurse who doesn't like coffee. Crazy, I know!" Jules continued, "You're not dating anyone are you? I'm ready to find me a real man. You know, there are plenty of dogs chasin', but no pedigrees, if you know what I mean."

Rae finally got a word in, "I have seen this one guy a couple of times. You know, you should come to Music and Brew night on Friday. Lots of single men come. Coffee and live bands, perfect combination."

Jules smirked, "That sounds like fun. Not my normal hang out, but what the heck. I'll be there."

Rae replied, "All right. See you then." Jules was still her same condescending self. Rae put her out of her mind. She couldn't wait to get back to Seth.

Rae bought two hot pretzels and a couple of icy bottles of root beer. On her way back to Seth she thought to herself how romantic it would be to come back to the park at night when the glowing bulb lights were lit, and the moon shined down on the river.

When Rae reached the bench, Seth stood to join her.

"Oh yeah. The park, a beautiful woman, pretzels and root beer? Best date ever!" he bragged. He kept her laughing as they enjoyed the food, making their way back to the beginning of the trail.

Seth said, "So, I will be pretty busy for the next few days getting my article put together, but can I see you again soon?"

Rae smiled, "I would love that. You know, scientific studies have shown that coffee boosts productivity, so you should probably have a cup of quality brew every morning."

Seth laughed his deep, sexy laugh and agreed, "Hey, if science says so."

When they reached The Big Brew, he offered, "I'll see you in the morning then." He pulled her into a steady, sweet hug and gave her a tight squeeze. He rested his chin on top of her head and spoke seriously, "Can't wait."

Rae instantly felt butterflies. She slid her arms around his waist, not wanting to let go.

"Alright, I better get going," he murmured. She felt his reluctance when he pulled back. He kissed her forehead.

Rae whispered good-bye, turned, and stepped into her shop. As she closed the door, she already couldn't wait to see Seth in the morning.

So caught up in her own head, she didn't even notice the bustle around her as she floated upstairs to her studio apartment. Her prized possession, a huge, black iron bed, took up most of the space. Thankfully, there was an old art deco style bathroom equipped with a decent shower, and an extra bonus was a stacked washer and dryer in her tiny closet. She happily went about her normal Sunday chores of laundry and reading various magazines and books. When she finished, she headed down for a sandwich.

It was already eight o'clock, and The Big Brew closed at nine on Sundays. There was only one customer, so she let Sarah and Quincy go early. By eight thirty, Rae was alone and tidying up. Surprisingly, the door jingled open at a quarter till nine. Sam Preston swayed on his feet as he ambled around. He was off duty, and Rae knew that he had probably been guzzling Jim Beam all day. He stumbled up to the counter and slid onto a stool. He reeked of liquor. Rae was more than ready for bed, but decided she better make him a cup of black coffee to help sober him up. "Rae Rae, my sweet Rae," Sam slurred.

She became vexed, "You need to stop saying that, Sam. I'm not anyone's Rae Rae."

He persisted, "You know how I feel about you Rae. You bring that sweetness around here and sit in my lap."

She raised her voice, "Sam! You better be glad we are alone. I wouldn't hesitate to sock you right in the damn nose if you said that in front of my customers!"

He got off the stool and prowled around the counter grumbling, "I've waited a long time for you Rae. I have been patient, but I'm done waiting."

Sam's eyes were wild and glassy. His breath stale. "Sam? What are you doing," she whispered. Fear caused bile to rise up into her throat, and she could taste it. He forced her into the back corner of the counter. He put his hand behind her right knee and slid it up to her backside, groping. She was disgusted.

Rae screamed, "Sam! Stop it! You don't want to do this!" His body was solid, and she was pinned, overpowered and violated. He succeeded in reaching his left hand under her shirt. He was too strong, got a hold of her bra and jerked it down to her waist, tearing the straps, and scratching the skin over her ribs.

Rae was in a panic, but remembered her self-defense class from eighth grade. She slammed her knee into his crotch with all her strength. He let out an animalistic noise, as his head flew forward hard into her right eye socket with a smack. He dropped to his knees. Rae was seeing stars and tears were forming in her eyes from the pain, but she managed to jump over Sam, who had curled up, rolling on the floor behind the counter. She grabbed her cell off the register and called Quincy.

He lived close and was there in minutes. He immediately noticed the right side of her face was shielded with an ice pack. Sam had passed out where he lay. Rae explained the terrifying ordeal, and after arguing, he finally convinced her to call the police. She didn't want to ruin Sam, but he had been so dangerous. She knew everyone would know something happened tomorrow when they saw the soon-to-be black eye.

Much to her surprise, Seth walked in the door, quickening his steps as he noticed something was wrong. He took in the scene, grasping her shoulders, "I just had to see you one more time tonight. What the hell happened? Are you okay? Is that Sam? Did he hit you?"

Rae managed, "It's okay. I promise I'll be fine. I'm so happy you are here."

Seth held her in his arms, anger bubbling. Quincy attempted to reassure him, "She's right. It's more what Sam didn't do. Rae laid him out flat, and his cop buddies will be here any minute to haul his sorry ass to the station."

The officers arrived and didn't seem surprised to find Sam in this state. They loaded him into an unmarked SUV, and offered to drive Rae to the emergency room, but she refused. Photos were taken of her red, swollen face and the officers assured her Sam wouldn't be back in her shop. Quincy followed them outside.

Seth gathered her up again and she swore again, "I promise I'm alright. I'm not normally alone with the door unlocked. Thank you for being here."

He kissed her forehead and they walked up front to say goodnight. He watched her lock up before heading home.

Rae fell onto her white down comforter around midnight, after an adequate dose of ibuprofen. She fell asleep as soon as it dulled the pain.

She woke up at five. Her alarm would be going off in twenty minutes, so she got on up to take more pain meds.

When she looked at her reflection in the bathroom mirror, it wasn't as bad as it could have been. There was a black crescent under her right eye, but the swelling was gone. She applied thick concealer and foundation to try and hide it the best she could. Her hands were a little shaky. She supposed she was still a bit unnerved. Rae had no idea what her customers would think. She felt a little proud of herself. She hadn't been totally helpless. Things would have gone a lot further if she hadn't known how to defend herself.

She slipped into black leggings, a long red tee and shearling boots. She threw her hair up in a messy bun and went down to open the shop.

Rae's jitters eased when Quincy arrived early. He picked his favorite station on satellite radio, and they performed a duet to Pumped Up Kicks as the coffee perked. Quincy put the first batch of bagels on display.

More officers than ever stopped in to check on Rae. Judging by how full the shop was by seven, word must've spread fast about her black eye and what went down. She was getting all sorts of sympathy.

Seth strolled in early, even though he should already be at the office, scanning the shop for Rae.

"She's in the kitchen putting more bagels in the oven," Quincy answered his unasked question.

Seth chuckled softly, slid onto a stool, and asked Quincy for a dark roast with cream and sugar.

When the door swung open, he stood and pulled her around the corner into the back hallway, assessing the bruise. His emotions were both rage and helplessness. He wished he could have been there for her sooner. He searched her eyes and briefly saw a glimpse of his future. He put his hands around her face and kissed her above the injured eye, taking great care to be gentle.

Rae teared up. When she buried her face in his chest, he wrapped his arms around her. By the way her shoulders heaved, he could tell she hadn't cried in a very long time. He placed his lips on top of her head, hoping to calm her.

"You're okay now, Angel. Let it go." He whispered into her hair.

When her sobs subsided, she pulled back slightly. She simply said, "Thank you."

"Thank me? Thank me for what? I want to kill Sam! I wasn't here to help you. You saved my life! I was out on a run while some drunk, low-life cop had his hands on you!"

Rae shook her head, whisked tears away with her fingertips, and said, "You precious man! I'm thanking you for being here now. I'm thanking you for letting me release everything inside, and especially for just holding me."

Seth held on tighter. He kissed the top of her head, and she leaned up and kissed his cheek.

"Come with me," she said. "Let's go check on the bagels."

She made him laugh and eased his temper. He followed her into the kitchen. Even though Rae had shown Seth her vulnerable side, she was still the strongest woman he had ever met.

Rae transferred the tray from the oven to the warmer. She gave Seth a too quick peck on the lips and pulled him back into the shop. He walked back around the counter and sat on the stool where he had left his coffee. Rae leaned on the counter opposite of him and laced her fingers with his.

Quincy grabbed the mug to refill it with hot coffee.

"So, Rae really slayed the dragon last night?" Seth asked.

Quincy nodded his head.

Rae laughed. "Yeah, my fight response kicked in." Then she became more serious. "Sam scared me, but he was drunk out of his mind. If he had tried that sober, I'm not sure what would have happened. Things might have been a lot worse."

Seth replied sternly, "You can't be here alone with the door unlocked ever again." He turned to Quincy. "Thank you for being here for

Rae." He held out his hand in her direction. "Give me your phone. I want you to have me on speed dial, just in case." He also sent her number to his cell. "I can't stay long. I'm working on my spread. I will be calling you," he declared.

She retorted, "Good! I want you to."

He raised her hand to his lips and kissed it saying, "Bye, Angel."

"Bye. Talk to you tonight."

Quincy said, "Geez. These last two weeks have been wild. And you two look like college kids in love. He might be a keeper. If things don't work out with you…" he winked.

Rae giggled and agreed, "Yeah. Terrible and amazing all wrapped up together."

Sarah came in at lunch and would be closing. Rae climbed the steps and curled up in bed by eight o'clock. She touched the circle under her eye and winced. She had been busy and forgot about the aching. Her phone buzzed and she picked it up off the pillow beside her. It was a text from Seth.

Can I call you?

Her fingers eagerly typed. **Please do.**

The phone rang within seconds. She answered in a sultry voice, "Hello handsome."

Seth let out a small deep groan, "Oh man, Rae. The things you do to me."

Rae was not experienced in flirting, but it was easy with Seth, and even easier over the phone. She coyly replied, "What? Little old me? I could stare at you all day."

Seth moaned. "Same here sweetheart. I'm actually visualizing you lying in bed, with a thin sheet draped over your silhouette and the glow of lamp light casting shadows on the walls. It'd be a beautiful photo."

Rae's intensity increased. "What are you wearing?"

Seth laughed. "Wow! You are on a roll tonight. We better stop this train fast. I would play along, but I'd be torturing myself."

She kept it going, "Some find a little torture pleasurable. How about you? What if I slid this thin sheet down a bit?"

Seth immediately became hard. "This could get pleasurably painful my dear. That would be a photo I would keep all to myself. We can continue this another time when you don't need to get some rest."

This time Rae laughed, "I know. I know. I've never had sexual play over the phone before, and it feels very liberating." She continued, more serious now, "Thank you for this morning. I needed to let go a little bit. It seems like you show up right when I need you."

Seth paused for a moment. "Just so you know, I went to The Book Bank the day I officially met you hoping to find you there. And I did…and I can't explain it, but…"

Rae stopped him. "You don't have to explain. Maybe we shouldn't try to explain it. Just know that feel the same. Now, what are you wearing?" She said teasing him.

Seth could only laugh with her.

"I hate to say it, but I really need some shut eye after the past couple of days. Plus, the sooner I go to sleep, the sooner it will be morning and I get to see your face walk through my door."

"You sure you're not up for company?" Seth sighed. "Sorry, I know. I'm being bad."

Damn, the thought made her tingle all over. She chastised herself internally, wishing she could say yes. "Tempting, but…"

"Sleep tight, my angel," he said in a silky voice.

Chapter Four

The rest of the week went on without a hitch. Seth came in every morning for coffee and flirting. He called her every night. Because he had to present his article at the office first thing Friday morning, he wouldn't be by for his daily dose of caffeine. He promised he would see her that night at Music and Brew. Rae scolded herself for already missing him so much. It would only be one morning without him, but it made her want him more.

Rae was up before the sun. She inspected her eye in the mirror and smiled, thankful her make up now hid the unsightly discoloration completely. She wanted to look extra sexy today. If Seth wasn't going to make the move to really kiss her, she had no problem doing it herself. She couldn't hold out any longer. She deep desires inside were too powerful to ignore.

After slipping a black, long-sleeved, v-neck T-shirt over hear head, she pulled on jeans that fit just right, accentuating one of her best assets. She put her hair up in a playful ponytail and bounced down the stairs. Sarah and Quincey harassed Rae all day long, making kissy faces at her.

The night came fast, and Music and Brew was almost in full swing. One of her favorite local bands was setting up on the stage toward the front of her shop. With the door propped open, people could stop and listen from the street. The smell of fresh coffee and warm apple pie always brought them on in. Quincy and Sarah were already serving some patrons who arrived early to sit at the small tables in front of the stage. Rae was busy in the kitchen setting out the pies she had baked after lunch.

She pulled out her phone to text Seth: **What's your favorite kind of pie?**

There was no reply. No less than five minutes later, the kitchen door swung open.

"Chocolate. Always chocolate," Seth said from behind a full bouquet of red roses.

Rae was thrilled. He looked very tasty. He had on the grey Henley from the day she met him and khakis. His five o'clock shadow was so masculine.

She took the roses and put them in an antique crock. "Seth, I love them! So, your meeting went well this morning?" she asked.

He followed her out of the kitchen, and she place the crock beside the register. "Yeah, it went great. They were impressed. I'll bring you a copy when it's printed."

Seth wanted to drag her up the stairs, and have a full on make out session, but he restrained himself, and sat on his usual stool while Rae went back to retrieve his pie.

Once the band finished their sound check, they slid right into R.E.M.'s "Losing My Religion." Seth turned to watch the door, amazed as more people filed in from the streets. He'd seen The Big Brew busy, but he didn't realize it would draw this kind of a crowd on a Friday night. A familiar face in a tight red mini dress, black stilettos, and matching cherry lips caught his eye. Not because he was attracted to her, but because he hadn't expected to see familiar faces after being in Austin for such a short time. And how could he not recognize Nurse Julie? When she saw him she stopped in her tracks, then noticeably adjusted her gait to a more seductive stride. As she approached, she flashed him brilliant smile, like a little girl who'd just found a pony under the Christmas tree.

"Seth Reagan!" She beamed as she looped her arm in his. "Did you lose my number? I've been waiting for you to call me."

Julie rubbed him the wrong way from the start, and her pathetic attempt at flirting now didn't quell those original feelings. "Well, I haven't had any questions. The stitches came out easily and I'm feeling myself again."

Jules laid it on thick, "I would have come to Rae Rae's place sooner if I had known you'd be here."

His eyebrows lifted. "Oh, you know Rae?"

She grinned. "Oh sure. I knew her in college. She was a little art nerd. The professor asked me to be the muse, you know—the model—on occasion. Rae was always in the library I think." Julie's dress traveled way too high up her thigh when she slid onto the stool next to Seth.

When Rae came out of the kitchen with Seth's pie, a look of surprise crossed her face, then was gone just as quickly. He stiffened. The last thing he wanted was for Rae to get the wrong impression with Jules cozied up to him. Seth reclaimed his arm and scooted up to his pie.

Julie's lips twisted. "You have any macaroons or petite fours?"

"No, Jules, only coffee, tea, bottled water and pie tonight. Nothing fancy." Rae's tone conveyed her annoyance.

"I'll just have water then. Thanks, Rae Rae."

Seth could see the irritation all over Rae's face. He winked at her. "Mmm, mmm this pie Rae! Did you put something extra in here? 'Cause I'm in love!"

Using humor to negate tension had always been his strong point. He hoped it was enough to bring Rae's good mood back. He didn't want Julie ruining an otherwise perfect evening.

The good music and crisp weather brought in more business than ever. It was standing room only by ten. The atmosphere was exciting. When the band took a short break, dance music poured from the speakers.

Since Seth refused to give her the attention she craved, he watched Julie move on to flirting with one of Quincy's young rugby teammates. When "Blurred Lines" started playing, she drew the boy to the dance floor. She moved provocatively, glancing at Seth to see if was watching. He couldn't have cared less and found it a little comical.

A giggle from behind him made him turn around. He and Rae shared a laugh, as he shook his head at the ridiculousness of Julie's attempt. Rae started singing to him along with the song. As she came around the counter, Seth had a feeling Julie could see the entire thing out of the corner of her eye.

Rae put her hands on Seth's knees, pulled his long legs apart, and slid in between them. Seth raised his thick, dark eyebrows, visibly surprised with the bold move. He loved it and was more than willing to play along. She slid her hands up his chest and around his neck. Seth's hands found the curve of her back. She pulled his lips down to hers. Her mouth was soft and tasted like whipped cream. He returned the kiss deeper for a better taste exploring with his tongue and the farce became beautiful reality.

When it ended, they were still forehead to forehead, out of breath and wanting more. Rae leaned back, but stayed in his personal space. He had a look in his eyes, and she knew what it meant.

"Quincy is closing tonight," she told him. "You've never seen my apartment. I'd love to show it to you later."

Seth cleared his throat. "Love to. Scientific studies have shown that being in a new environment boosts productivity, so yeah."

Rae laughed sweetly and squeezed his knees. "We can get very creative," she said with light in her eyes.

Seth ran a hand through his hair and licked his lips, where the taste of whipped cream still lingered. Rae turned around, leaned back on his chest. Across the room, Seth noticed Jules sporting a pouty look. Rae had definitely staked her claim on him. He could tell by the satisfaction in her confident posture.

Seth toyed with Rae's ponytail to distract himself from her being in such close proximity, and the tingling he was feeling down below. The golden strands felt like satin and smelled of cinnamon. The band returned and slowed things down with Stone Temple Pilots "Adhesive." Seth pushed the ponytail aside and whispered into her ear, "Dance with me, Angel."

At his insistence, Rae pulled him to the floor to join the other couples. He slid his hands around her waist and leaned down into her. Rae had never felt more sensual as she did swaying with Seth, feeling his heat and his fingers caressing her hips. She didn't realize dancing could be such erotic foreplay. She couldn't hold out much longer. Her body was demanding gratification. Seth's heart was pounding against hers, and his breath had escalated. He felt like they were melding into one aroused being. This amorous undulating was almost as satisfying as the sexual act itself, but he needed to appease the beckoning of her body. They were tumbling over the edge together and needed to ditch the crowd.

They abandoned the dance floor and hurried upstairs.

Seth eased the door shut behind them and locked it. He felt wild inside. Rae's apartment was small, the bed was no more than five steps from the door. She sat on the edge and began unlacing her boots. Seth offered to take over the task. She leaned back on her palms, without taking her eyes from him she watched his deft hands work. He removed each one slowly and threw them at the door with a clunk. He paused for a moment to absorb her alluring stare. Electricity buzzed between them. He became obsessed with the primitive need to consume her.

Rae stood up and slowly slid his shirt off, cherishing every second. His form was magnificent, and his skin was firm and smooth. She made a circle around the bullet wound with her fingers. When she looked up into his eyes, her pulse quickened.

Seth was boiling inside, and when Rae licked her lips, he responded expeditiously. He clasped his hands around her waist and seized her mouth with his. Their kisses felt desperate. He unfastened her jeans and slid them to the floor, as Rae jerked her shirt over her head.

He eased down to sit on the bed and lured her to straddle his hips. She was wearing a black lace thong, and he clenched her bottom in his grip as they continued to taste each other. He mumbled, "Oh god Rae you're sexy."

She smiled wickedly and held his face in her hands, feeling the roughness of his cheeks, while she continued to feast on his desire.

She arched into his body, and he slid his skillful fingers between her legs. She was undone. She let out a pleading moan and writhed against his actions. He didn't stop until she shuddered and closed her mouth over his shoulder to muffle her cry of pleasure.

He had given her an intimate gift and she was burning to fulfill his fleshly needs. She kept her lips on his shoulder then trailed kisses up to the hollow of his neck. He let out an ardent groan and removed her matching lace bra. She took it from his hands and began winding it around his wrists. "Who's sexy now? All tied up with lace," she teased.

Seth looked at her with excitement. He didn't know he could be more aroused than he already was. Rae raised his hands above his head, and pushed him back on the bed, still straddling him. She held him captive and wanted his body to beg for release. She devoted herself to his pleasure. Her right hand held his wrists down. Her left hand traced along his brow. Light fingertips fluttered across his cheek and then his lips. She placed her hand over his throat and began kissing his mouth. His hips raised against her. Seth wouldn't hold out much longer.

He sat up, threw his bound hands behind her back, pulled her against his chest, and ravaged her for more. When he couldn't stand to wait another second, he stood, and Rae took off his remaining clothes. She untied the lacy restraint. He threw her down on the bed, retrieved a condom from the pocket of his pants now lying on the floor, and covered her with his long body. Rae clasped her legs around his hips again, and he was inside her. He moved slow at first.

It had been a long time since either had been with anyone. They had both imagined this moment, but no expectations could compare. The feeling of being inside her was enchanting. When he was at the peak of indulgence,

"Take me." Rae whispered, looking deep into his eyes. "I'm yours." At those words he surrendered to her in rapture. His breath was ragged, and Rae had a feeling of complete contentment.

He propped up over her on one arm and studied the shape of her body. Like a photograph, he wanted her image burned into his mind. Rae started to giggle.

"Why are you laughing?" he asked in a husky voice.

"I'm laughing at all my glorious nakedness you seem to be perusing."

He laughed, and traced a finger over her hip, "Oh woman, I'm supposed to be boosting productivity, so I'm getting to know my subject."

Rae asked, "Have I worn you out?"

Seth sat up straight and rubbed his hand down her hair. "I'm far from worn out, but a shower would be nice. Can I wash your hair?"

Rae gave a shy nod and led him into the bathroom.

For the next half hour, they washed each other's hair and discussed the intoxicating smell of her organic shampoo. Rae giggled each time Seth kissed a new spot on her shoulder, hip or neck. When they were dry again, the coffee shop had closed. There wasn't a sound coming from downstairs.

"I have a question, but I already know the answer." Rae said.

Seth raised a brow.

"Chocolate, always chocolate," she said.

Seth showed his perfect white teeth with a big grin. "You and I are on the same page," he said with a mischievous look in his eyes. He pulled on his boxer briefs and pants and Rae wrapped a light pink satin robe around herself. They sneaked down the steps as though they were going on an adventure.

Rae laid a fresh tablecloth on the stage. They downed glasses of milk and devoured the pie. Seth had awakened something inside Rae she had never known before. Seth licked the pie off his fingers. He wasn't trying to be sexy, but Rae was wishing she had brought out the whipped cream. He made her more daring, naughty even. They were so comfortable with each other. Seth could walk into a room and everyone noticed him, and for some cosmic reason, he chose her out of the many available women around. The chemistry was palpable between them.

After clearing the dishes, Seth coaxed Rae out of the kitchen and onto the bottom step. He sat down and pulled her in his lap. He enclosed her in his arms, leaned down, forehead to forehead, and said, "This…night…was…epic."

Rae giggled. "Wow. You know how to make a girl feel good."

Seth rubbed a hand up and down her back, and deepened his voice. "I'm serious. I'm under your spell."

She kissed him sensuously. He was the best kisser. She sighed to herself, and asked, "Is this goodnight?"

He didn't answer. He didn't want to say yes. His green eyes were heavy and Rae whispered, "Stay with me?"

He scooped her up with ease and carried her upstairs. They crawled into bed, and she slept with her head on his heart.

When Rae woke the next morning, Seth was no longer beside her. There was a single rose lying on the cool pillow beside her with a note that read:

> Good morning beautiful. Just needed to change clothes. I'll be back in an hour for my morning coffee. There should be a brew called
>
> Black Lace! XOXO

Rae's heart did a flip, and she laughed out loud at his clever coffee joke. Extremely good looking, successful, caring, and funny. She didn't know how she had gotten so lucky. Last night had been the best night of her life, hands down. Rae hopped out of bed, excited to start a new day.

Chapter Five

Seth grabbed his laptop and his keys and was almost out the door when his cell phone rang. It was his older brother Clay.

"Hey man. Sorry it's so early. Um, I'm calling about dad. He's been having some abdominal pain and other issues for quite some time, but of course hadn't mentioned it to anyone. A specialist did tests and…and found a tumor in his colon. He took a biopsy. It's cancer. He is scheduled for surgery to remove it Monday morning. Mom wanted me to break the news. I know you're probably busy…"

"No. No, I'll be there. Clay, tell dad I'll be there. Tell them both I love them."

Seth was in shock, but Dad had always kept his problems out of sight from the family. Maxwell Raegan never failed to be the alpha of the household, and took care of any issues behind the scenes. In a way, Seth appreciated that about his father, but he also knew his mother longed to be included in sharing the burden of daily life. Dad viewed it as protecting her. He knew Mom just wished she could be more of a support for him.

He shot a quick text to Rae.

Angel, I have to get to Utah for a short time. Dad's sick. Not sure when I'll be back. I will miss you badly. XOXO

Seth caught the first flight home. He expected his brother Clay to be waiting at the baggage claim, but he was nowhere in sight. As Seth pulled his duffle bag from the conveyor belt, he heard a familiar voice behind him. "Mr. Reagan, your chariot awaits."

He turned to see Claire Valentine, his ex-girlfriend he'd split with just before he moved to Austin. She was his sister's best friend, so she would always be close to the family.

Claire was tall, and too thin since he had last seen her. She was very pale with copper red hair that hung down to her waist. She looked like a model and was told her entire life how stunning she was. She tried to be soothing, "I knew Clay and everyone else would be busy, so I offered to bring you home." Seth just wanted to get to his parent's house as quickly as possible. He was polite. "Thank you. I'm anxious to talk to

Dad. I'm a little pissed he didn't let us know what was going on," he said. She put her arm through his and they proceeded to her car. Claire kept the conversation light on the ride home. She was aware of his agitation. It was raining and matched Seth's gloomy mood. She asked about his new job and about Austin. He only answered in fragments. He didn't tell her about the mugging or that he had been shot. He hadn't told anyone in his family. They were known worriers, and after the news this morning, he was glad they never knew.

They arrived at the Reagan house at noon. Mom greeted them on the front porch of the large brick house. Seth's older brother Clay, and Jenny, his younger sister each had their own rooms in the big colonial. The house held the familiar smell of bread baking. Seth knew exactly where his father would be. Dad stood from his recliner, and was embraced in a bear hug from Seth. All frustration faded away, as the reality of what would happen the next day settled in.

Claire and Eva went to the kitchen to make lunch. The four of them ate in the living room around the tv while Seth spoke a little bit about his new job, and the great views of Austin from his apartment. He brought out his laptop and showed them the photos he had taken at Lady

Bird Lake. He quickly scrolled through a few of Rae standing by the water, so he wouldn't have to explain who she was just yet.

The rest of the family showed up in a short time, and Eva made a huge Italian feast. The family had requested her specialty spaghetti and meatballs.

After dinner, Seth avoided Claire by playing with his nieces and nephews. The children's bedtime came, and Clay and Jenny left with their families. They would all be meeting at the hospital first thing in the morning.

Seth reluctantly walked Claire out to her car. She leaned on the black BMW, obviously not ready to leave. He wasn't ready to get into hurt feelings and deep regrets with her tonight.

"Thank you, again," he said. Then glanced over his shoulder toward the house. "I gotta get up early so…"

She put her hand on his crossed arm. Her eyes were pleading with him, but she said nothing. She raised on her tiptoes and planted a kiss on his lips. She let go and quickly got in her car and pulled off.

Seth was dazed. She didn't give him a chance to say a word. The kiss confirmed he had no desire for her anymore. He felt nothing when she kissed him. He needed to sit her down and have a talk, but that would have to wait.

Seth sent a quick text to Rae, along with the picture he took of them the day they went to the river.

Made it home. Missing you. XOXO

He went to sleep thinking about the night before. The passion they had found in each other had Seth enamored with her. He couldn't wait to dream about his angel.

The surgery went as smoothly as possible. The whole family was waiting in Dad's room when the nurse wheeled him in on the hospital bed. He was fast asleep, but looked well. He would be staying at least three days, maybe more.

Seth shot Rae a text on Monday.

Dad had surgery. All is well, for now. Miss you. Talk to you soon. XOXO

Dad went home after four days which was cause for celebration. The pathology report had shown no evidence of cancer outside of the tumor. There was no need for chemotherapy since surgery was curative. The family gathered once again around the long farmhouse table.

Claire quickly claimed the seat next to Seth, and began laying on the charm. Seth tried to ignore her advances, despite her persistence. They knew each other intimately for five years, and she could tell he was trying to avoid her. He had given her none of his time while he was in town, and zero attention when she visited Jenny. Claire came by the house every day, but Seth managed to have plans elsewhere when she came around. He couldn't give her an inch and would not be caught alone with her. Now, he was stuck right beside her.

She leaned in close, touching her elbow to his. She crossed her legs and let her foot graze his leg. Seth let out an audible sigh, shaking his head. His family could tell by the look on his face that he had had enough. Seth was the first up to clear the table.

Jenny joined him in the kitchen. "Seth, I'm worried about Claire."

He let out another big sigh as he roughly rinsed the dishes in the sink. "And this is my problem, why?"

Jenny leaned on the counter next to him. "I don't think she's eating. Like, nothing. She's so skinny. She's not over you, Seth."

He pondered her words. "You mean she's depressed?"

"Yes," Jenny answered.

"Have you tried to talk to her about it?"

Jenny shrugged her shoulders. "Sort of, but she always says she's just dieting. She still talks about marrying you, Seth."

He clanked the dishes in the sink with frustration trying not to get too loud. "You and I both know that's never going to happen. I mean, I don't know what you want me to do. I know we were together for what seems like forever, but everything has changed. My life is moving forward, but she obviously is not. I'm seeing someone," he said and couldn't help but smile.

Jenny smiled back, intrigued. "Oh, really? I can't even imagine you with another girl on your arm. She's not a redhead, is she?"

He laughed. "No. She's perfect. Her hair's like honey and she's just as sweet," he said blushing.

Jenny gave him a hug and said, "Good. I promise I'm happy for you."

Seth said quietly, "I'll try to talk to Claire."

When they came out of the kitchen, the others were gathering up to leave. Claire grabbed Seth's arm and said, "Walk me out."

Neither uttered a word until they reached her car, and had watched everyone else go. "Claire…" Seth started.

"Wait." She stopped him. "I miss you. I've been a mess since you left, and I keep thinking you'll be back, but…" She looked desperate.

"Claire," he said firmly, but calmly. "I'm not moving back. My life is in Austin now."

She interrupted again, "I could come there."

He almost shouted, "No, Claire!"

She had tears in her eyes. She grabbed his face and kissed him hard. He pulled away and started for the door to the house. When he reached the porch he turned and said, "That's not happening again. I'm leaving tomorrow afternoon. Goodbye Claire."

And with that, he went inside. He had nothing more to say.

Seth knew it was late, but it was Saturday night. Maybe Rae was still up. He felt bad that he hadn't talked to her all week. He decided to call her just to see. Her phone rang and rang, then went to voicemail. He didn't leave a message. He knew he would see her the following night, and he would apologize face to face.

Then he sent a text to Claire. He hated leaving her in tears, but she wasn't listening to what he was telling her. She needed to accept realty and move on.

Rae had been down in the dumps for days. She really didn't understand why she hadn't heard from Seth. She decided she would take it up with him in person if he ever came back. She was feeling like she had been a one night stand the way things were going. Tomorrow was her day off, and she scheduled herself a massage to ease her stress. She and Quincy closed up and she got into bed at eleven. She glanced at her cell. Nothing. No calls. No texts. She turned it on vibrate and went to sleep.

Rae woke up late. She hadn't set an alarm, and her massage wasn't until noon. When she picked up her phone, there was a text. It was from Seth.

I'm sorry I just left you the way I did, but we can't do this. Things have changed. You need to find someone new, and I'm not an option. Again, I'm sorry.

Rae was completely dumbfounded. She felt like a piano had fallen out of the sky and landed right on top of her head. She was angry and hurt. She quickly shot a text back and threw her phone into her bag.

Seth was packing his things when his cell signaled he had gotten a message. It was only two words.

ROYAL ASSHOLE

And it was from Rae. Seth was confused for two seconds, then realized what he had done.

Seth tried to call, but Rae had left her phone at home. He couldn't imagine what she must be thinking. He sent her a text in hopes that she would see it before he could get to her.

I made a huge mistake!!! I will explain everything, but that text was NOT for you! Cross my heart. I've been dying to get back to you. Please believe me. My plane arrives at noon, and I'm coming straight to The Big Brew.

Chapter Six

Rae almost cancelled her massage appointment to wallow in self-loathing, but went on. It could only help, right? When she checked in at the reception desk, the clerk informed her that Sebastian would be her massage therapist.

Rae laid on the table face down with only a heavy white blanket covering her from the waist down. The room was dark and smelled of sandalwood and cloves. She would never understand why they combined waves crashing with what seemed like sounds you would hear in outer space, but she was oddly comforted.

Rae heard the door open and close. She could only see the floor below her. Sebastian slid the blanket between her legs. Keeping her bottom unexposed. Two large, warm hands swept from her toes all the way to her thighs. Being touched by a man's hands made her instantly think of Seth.

A voice as deep as melted dark chocolate said, "If I work to light or too deep, please let me know."

Rae replied, "You're great. It's great. Thank you." As she lay there, trying to relax, various ways to tell Seth off ran through her mind. She had a feeling the anger would dissipate as soon as she saw his face. Sebastian retrieved her from her thoughts, when he asked that she flip over to her back. Rae turned over and closed her eyes. She practiced deep breathing to clear her mind and enjoyed the rest of the massage.

She felt calm, cool and collected as she walked back to The Big Brew. She paused before entering the shop. Seth was inside pacing back and forth in long strides in front of the green couch. He sensed her, halted and turned to peer out of the window. They kept coming back to this place, gazing at each other through the window.

This time Rae's eyes were cold and it pained Seth to his core. He noticed she sighed heavily as she came through the door.

Rae noticed he looked tired and stressed, and asked in a frustrated tone, "Can I help you with something? Is your father ok?" She avoided looking into his eyes, trying her best to act angry.

Seth ran his hand through his hair, "Yes. Dad's fine. I need to talk to you Rae. This is important. You are important to me Rae. I made a mistake"

She kept walking through the shop and up the stairs. He trailed behind her, and she let him, because she didn't want to make a scene in front of her customers. She smelled his soap, and struggled to stay mad as they entered her room. Rae threw her bag on the dresser, walked into her bathroom, and shut the door behind her.

Seth eased down onto the edge of the bed. He had no idea what was about to happen. He knew he couldn't lose her. He knew he wouldn't leave her room until he had her forgiveness.

Rae examined herself in the mirror, and whispered a string of profanities because she knew she didn't have the will power to fend off the irresistible man on the other side of the door. She slid out, and stayed leaned against the bathroom door. She crossed her arms, and almost melted seeing his eyebrows knit together.

Seth couldn't keep the distance between them and came to stand close in front of her. He gave a half smile and said, "You look great. I missed you more than you know."

She started to speak, but he placed a finger on her lips.

"I didn't call you. I should have. I can't change it now. That text mix-up was a nightmare. I have to explain or I'll explode."

Rae looked up at him, butting in, "I want you to explain, or I'll be in a constant state of pissed off, but maybe we should slow down a bit. Maybe we let things happen too fast."

Seth nodded. He was going to let her have control of the conversation, as long as it was mending the relationship. She didn't waver yet, "Continue."

He sat back down and leaned on his knees to resist the urge to pull her into his lap and hold on.

"Dad had major surgery for colon cancer, but they got all of the tumor out. The days that followed seemed to go by so fast. I know you aren't upset with me for being there for my family. I know not hearing from me all week and getting that terrible message must have blindsided you. When I realized the huge mistake I made, my heart shattered. That text was meant for Claire. She showed up the first day I was home, depressed and being very obsessive. She wanted things to go back to the way they were before I left Utah. Believe me, I tried my best to make it clear that wasn't going to happen. I told my family that I'm seeing someone, and I pray that's still the case. I want you to meet them," he said softly. He held up his hand, "In the future. I know, slow."

His eyes were intense, and she sensed his need for her presence. She felt like a magnet was pulling her to him. She closed the space between them. He grasped her around the waist and buried his head in her stomach. She ran her hands through his hair. His deep voice vibrated into her tummy.

"Thank you. Thank you. Just hold on to me, Angel." Rae leaned down to kiss the top of his head. She forgave him. She knew she would. Her soul found peace in his arms, and her body was responding. She needed to lighten the heaviness and stay away from getting physical.

"Have you had anything to eat lately?' she asked. Seth shook his head no. "Let me make you a sandwich. Okay?" She reluctantly stepped back one step and looked into his puppy dog eyes. He knew what he was doing to her.

She laughed and said, "Dammit, I can't even attempt to stay mad at you!"

Seth stood to tower over her. He held her face in his hands and said, "Good, I have you where I want you then."

They laughed together. He continued, "Seriously though, I didn't mean to hurt you. I hate myself for doing it."

She replied, "Good. Don't do it again."

After eating, Rae walked Seth to the front door. He thanked her for the food, and for her forgiveness. He gathered her up in a bear hug.

"Text me to let me know you got home, ok?" she said.

"I will. Can I come in for coffee in the morning?" he asked.

She gave him a big smile, "Please do. Can I join you?"

"Of course!"

He stepped outside and kept his eyes locked onto hers. She reached up to lock the door, but opened it instead. In one long stride, he grabbed onto her and kissed her deeply. They couldn't separate without it. He let go and she slipped back inside, locking the door this time. He was still staring. They both smiled and laughed at each other through the glass door. He motioned for her to go upstairs and blew her a kiss. Rae walked up the stairs to her apartment feeling like all was right in the world. She felt like their relationship had been reborn. She slept like a baby that night.

Chapter Seven

It was Monday. Rae was up by five. Seth had come in before work, and it was like they didn't skip a beat. He had been gone for over a week and decided to drive out to McKinney Falls to get working on his next project. The day was busy and went by quickly. Rae would be off at six, and Seth had asked her to dinner at his place. He said they needed to have a real date, and planned on wining and dining her.

Rae shimmied into a knee-length black lace dress, and green kitten heels. When she slowly came down the steps to avoid falling, Sarah and Quincy stood, mouths gaping in silence. Rae snapped her fingers in Quincy's face, and he looked over to Sarah.

"Damn!" They said in unison.

Rae smiled. "Perfect! That's what I'm going for."

They heard a loud sound and something caught Rae's eye. It was Seth on a black, rumbling motorcycle pulling up in front of The Big Brew. She had no idea he drove a motorcycle, but that made him even more appealing. He swung his long leg over the bike, and walked over to the big window. He pulled out a magazine from inside his black leather jacket, and held it up to the glass. She walked over to see. It was his article. The page was filled with gorgeous photographs of her shop. She had never felt so special. She kissed her fingertips, pressed them to the glass, and tilted her head towards the door.

Seth walked in and handed it to her.

"I'll frame it! This is the best, Seth!"

He shook his head. "This dress is the best!"

She looked down. "Yeah, maybe not the best for riding a motorcycle. Should I change?"

"Please don't. You know how I feel about black lace. Especially on you." Her face reddened. Not because of what Seth said, but because she was wearing a red lace thong. They had agreed to slow down, but they both knew that would not be the case.

Seth drove them a few minutes to his AMLI South Shore apartment on Riverside Drive. Rae had always wanted to see the inside of this building. The lobby was bright, and very modern with mid-century style furnishings. As soon as they stepped into the elevator, Seth intertwined his fingers with hers.

"I didn't like being away from you, Rae" he told her. His tone held a singe of heat that sent a tingle from her head to her toes.

They arrived on the fifth floor and entered the luxury apartment. Moody music was playing. The first thing Rae noticed was a wall of windows that opened to a beautiful view of Lady Bird Lake. The glistening lights of the city were reflecting on the water. She let out a small gasp, as he led her out onto the balcony. She leaned on the rail, and Seth came in behind her, and wrapped his arms around her.

He whispered, "I'm so happy to finally be home with you."

"Home"

Seth saying that simple word burned into her soul.

She was instantly turned on. He smelled so good. Rae had bought Irish Spring to have his scent around all the time. Just when she started to imagine all of the things she wanted to do to him, he stepped away and went inside. She turned to watch him as he opened the fridge and began setting out beautiful plates of sushi rolls onto the large granite island.

She stepped back inside, removed her heels, and joined him at the counter. Seth pulled out a bottle of chilled plumb wine, and generously poured it into two stemmed glasses.

"You weren't kidding about the wining and dining," she said. "You made this? It's not take out?"

He dropped his jaw playing with her. "Yes! I made it! I spent two weeks in Kyoto a couple of years ago. Japan has the most amazing temples. I'll show my pictures sometime. Anyway, it was me and my dad. He had worked with the owners of the Hotel Okura, and I had the privilege of spending my nights in the kitchen with the chef. I've been practicing, but you are the lucky first to sample my handiwork."

He just kept surprising her. He hadn't set a table. Instead, he picked her up by the waist, and easily sat her on top of the counter beside the food. He hopped up to sit next to her. They shared the tuna, crab and avocado rolls, and sipped their wine. It was perfect.

"I'm going to go back one day. You should come with me. I mean, we'll have to wait at least a year until I have vacation time built up."

Rae was a little taken aback. "A year? You plan on keeping me around that long, huh?"

Seth took her wine and sat both glasses down. He leaned in and pulled her hand to his cheek. "I do. Is that ok with you?"

Rae was thrilled. He kissed the inside of her wrist, and her head began to spin. She almost couldn't speak.

"Seth, I think I would go anywhere with you. Today or ten years from now."

He didn't hesitate. He kissed her. He kissed her with more passion than he had ever felt before. They were both panting when it ended, and they began to laugh. Rae loved it that they laughed in moments like this. They enjoyed each other.

"More wine?" Seth asked.

"Absolutely," she replied grinning.

He slid off the counter and poured the glasses full. He led her to the brown leather sofa where he sat, and she nestled next to his side with his arm around her shoulders.

"I was serious about you meeting my family, and it may be sooner rather than later," he said.

She snickered. "Well, may as well, since I'm going to be around for a while."

He laughed his deep sexy laugh. "My parents want to come here for Thanksgiving. Maybe you could join us?" He knew she didn't have holiday plans, and there was no one he would rather be with.

"What about the rest of them, your sister, your brother and their kids?"

"I'm not positive, but they probably will go wherever Mom and Dad are."

Rae said, "Here? You're going to have everyone here? You don't even have a dining table." He looked deep in thought and said, "Hmm. You're right. I'll just have to get one."

"Or..." Rae said. "We could have everyone over to The Big Brew?"

Seth raised his thick dark brows she adored.

She continued, "It's perfect! Cook the turkey and all the fixins in the kitchen. Push the tables into one long one. The kids can play on the stage, and I have been wanting to put up a big flat screen. We can watch football..."

His excitement showed on his face. "I can't think of a better place for us to be. Do you know how amazing you are?" He practically growled into her ear.

The song "I Only Have Eyes For You" began floating through the air. Seth stood, and pulled Rae to her feet. He snaked an arm around her waist and started to sway. She looked serious and asked,

"You sure you want to do this?" His eyes answered yes. She continued, her eyes bright, "You really want to do this, cause if we slow dance to this, it will be our song, like, forever."

He grinned. "Positive."

They were nose to nose, and Rae was smoldering. She leaned up, and whispered in his ear, "I missed you so much. I want you badly." She kissed his neck.

"Slow, huh?" he asked.

"We can take our time," she purred.

He backed her up to the wall next to the huge window. He pinned her against it as he began devouring her neck. He would definitely describe her as savory. His hands were enticing her to respond as he moved them up under her dress. He found the cool smooth skin of her bottom. The warmth of his palms caused her to shiver. His fingertips touched the lace at the top curve of her buttock, and he looked down to see the red thong.

"Red," he growled. "Oh, Rae you're killing me." He didn't want to strip her down in front of the window, so he pulled her dress back down, threw her over one shoulder, and took her into his bedroom.

She made no protest. She couldn't wait to be intimate with Seth again. He let her down to her feet, and they both undressed in less than a minute. Neither of them had a stitch of clothing on. He wound his arms around her waist and lifted her up so that her feet were not touching the floor. She wrapped her legs around his waist. They locked eyes, face to face, chest to chest. He easily held her against the wall and, with one smooth move they were unified. He gripped her hips with his long fingers and kissed her like it was the end of the world. His mouth moved to feast on her neck, while he simultaneously guided her up and down, his hips pushing into her with each perfectly timed movement. His hard abdomen hit her in just the right spot. More than ready to soar into another dimension, she arched her back, offering herself up to him. He sped up the pace, both moaning with pure pleasure, and concluded with a shudder. Rae did not stifle her divine lamentation. Seth leaned against her, breathless.

His angel had quenched his scorching want. She held on as he walked backwards, and eased back onto the bed, so that her body laid on top of his.

Seth let out a short laugh and said, "I bet we woke Lucy up."

Rae giggled. "Oops."

"She's been conveniently leaving her apartment when I leave mine. She likes to do her yoga right down by the lake where I can see. I bet she'll understand that I'm not interested after tonight."

Rae rubbed her palm over his stubbled cheek. "Look at you. Can you blame her?"

She was feeling sweaty, so she rolled onto the bed. The gray comforter was thick, soft and smelled like Seth. He got up and pulled on a pair of sweatpants. He leapt over her like a pouncing lion, nuzzled her ear and whispered, "Stay put. I'll be right back."

Rae sat up when he went towards the kitchen. His closet door was open, so she retrieved a soft green, worn out tee that said Zion National Park, and tugged it over her head.

Seth came back with a bottle of water and a box of Godiva truffles. His fire was re-ignited when he saw her laying on his bed, wearing his tee. He held up the box. "I hope these are acceptable. I didn't learn to make dessert sushi. Yet."

Rae nodded with a sweet smile. "You can't go wrong with truffles. You make the sushi, and I will take care of dessert."

He stretched out beside her. "Great plan."

After emptying half the box, they both knew the night was coming to an end. It was only ten, but both had to be up early in the morning for work. Rae hung the tee back in the closet, and they redressed. Seth couldn't help himself and continued kissing the back of her neck when they stepped inside the elevator. Rae's cell rang.

It was Quincy, and he sounded concerned. "Rae, when I was closing up, Sam pulled up across the street. He parked and sat there. I was curious, so after about an hour, I went back past the shop, and he's still there. It's like he's waiting for you to show up. Like he's watching you or something. I didn't call the cops, but I don't think you should come home alone."

Seth could tell from her expression that it was serious. The elevator door opened on the first floor, and Rae pushed the button to go back up to the fifth.

"I'm with Seth now and I'm pretty sure I can convince him to let me stay at his place tonight," she told Quincy. "I'll be fine. I won't go back tonight. Maybe you can meet me there to open up, and I'll let you off early tomorrow?"

He was always flexible. "You bet. No problem. Be happy to," Quincy said.

She was relieved. "If anything else happens, we can get the police involved. Good night, and thanks so much."

Seth had figured out Rae was staying the night, but wasn't sure why. They stepped out of the elevator, and Seth grabbed her hand, stopping in front of his door.

"It's Sam, isn't it?" Seth asked.

"Yeah, Quincy said he thinks he's been watching me, and is waiting for me to go back to my place."

"Rae, I can go take care of this right now," he said, his anger evident in his clenched fists.

"No way, Seth. Sam has guns, and I'm sure he keeps one in his car. I will call the police. I just didn't want Quincy going back down there. We'll let them take care of him."

They went back inside and Rae made the call. They told her to come by the station to file an order of protection.

Seth motioned for her to stay inside. He walked out onto the balcony to look around, feeling a little paranoid. When he came back in Rae's eyes glistened with the beginning of tears.

"I'm so sorry you are in the middle of all this." Her frustration was starting to show. "I mean, you get shot the first time you see me. Then, I get attacked at the shop, and now I'm forcing you to let me stay over. I'm always playing the victim to you and I don't like it."

Seth grabbed her shoulders firmly, and furrowed his brows, "Victim? The first time I saw you, you kept me from bleeding out on the sidewalk. Do you remember that? You defended yourself when that bastard tried to force himself on you. You are a strong, gorgeous woman who has cast a spell on me." He pulled her close against himself. "I've never wanted a woman more than I want you. I need you and I want you next to me in my bed tonight."

His arms. Seth's warm, strong, sexy arms were now turning her on again, while feeling like home at the same time. Rae let out the breath she had been holding in and relaxed a little.

"Ok. Can I sleep in your shirt?" she asked meekly.

Seth looked down at her with deep affection, laced with desire. "Every night, if you want."

She held his face and gave him a soft kiss. They could have easily went for round two, but both were content to just be there for each other.

Chapter Eight

The next morning there was no sign of Sam when they arrived at The Big Brew. It was only five, and the sun was not up yet. Quincy was there inside like he promised. Seth grabbed his coffee to go and went to the office early. After the lunch rush had dwindled down, Rae headed to the police station, and filed the protection order for herself and Seth. She wouldn't allow Seth to get hurt because of her. The cops told her they would serve the order to Sam as soon as they located him. He had left The Big Brew before they had arrived that night.

Getting back to work helped , but she felt a little on edge every time the door opened after dark. She also couldn't help from walking up to the front window every ten minutes to look for any sign of Sam. Sarah and Quincy usually closed the place down at nine during the week, but Rae had let Quincy leave early for helping her open. Sarah cleaned the big window, and smiled at Seth when he walked in at 8:45. Rae felt butterflies when she saw him.

"I'm so happy to see you," she said. Without uttering one word he bent down and kissed her passionately, holding on tightly.

Sarah smiled and said," I think I'll head out."

Seth loosened his embrace, but kept her close.

"Ok, Sarah. See you tomorrow. Be careful."

Seth tucked a strand of hair behind her ear, "I won't stay long. You need to get some rest. I just wanted to check the block and watch you lock up."

Rae wished he would stay, but she absolutely needed sleep, "It means the world to me," she said. They walked to the front door still stuck to one another.

"You be safe," she told him earnestly.

"I will see you in the morning, and then I'll be at the office all day, so if you need me, I can get here quick." She pulled his mouth down to hers and kissed him fervently, then locked the door behind him.

Things seemed to fall back into routine the following days, which made Rae happy. Friday came around fast, and Rae was glad it was

Music and Brew night. Having lots of people around helped her feel somewhat back to normal, and less tense. It was the season for pumpkin and caramel pie, so she was making sure she had plenty on hand. To keep drama at bay, she spent her time in the kitchen the duration of the morning baking.

Little did she know drama had just walked through the front door in the form of Claire Valentine. She had come to Austin seeking out Seth, and just so happened to stop in Rae's place for coffee. She was practically living off coffee these days. Quincy had a thing for red heads, male or female, and nearly tripped over himself to attend to her. She sat on the couch in the front of the store.

Seth sat in front of his Mac editing photos of McKinney Falls when he got a call from his sister Jenny. "Hey Sis. What's up?"

She paused, "So you haven't seen her yet I'm guessing."

Seth sat up straight, "Who? What's going on Jen?"

She began, "Seth, Claire is in Austin. She literally just sent me a text saying she had arrived about an hour ago. I can't believe she'd just show up like that."

Seth didn't know what to make of it, "Ok. Umm…I'm positive she doesn't know where my apartment is, but I'm sure she could find out where I work if she tried. Did you have any idea she was going to do this?" he asked on edge.

"No. No way Seth!" she answered.

He thought for a moment, "Does she know anything about Rae?"

"Not a thing," she replied firmly. "I would never talk about your relationships with her. I haven't seen much of Claire since you left, and now she won't reply to my texts. I'm trying to ask her where she's at now, and what she thinks she is going to do."

Seth said, "Well, keep trying. I will let Rae know what's going on. We need to talk more about Rae later. Love you sis."

"Ok. I will let you know if I can get her. You stay safe. Love you brother."

Seth shot a text to Rae, and carefully walked through the building. He was expecting to turn a corner, or enter the elevator and see Claire there, but it was all clear. He headed to The Big Brew.

Rae had taken four apple pies out of the oven when she got his text.

Claire is in Austin. I'm not sure where, but I think she needs to see us together. This has to stop. I'll be over in a few. XOXO

Rae was a little alarmed, but comforted with the knowledge that Seth was hers, and he was willing to defend their relationship. She had no idea why, but she also felt bad for Claire in a way.

When she stepped out of the kitchen, and stood behind the counter, she knew Claire Valentine was walking towards her. She was pale, gaunt looking and at least three inches taller than Rae.

"How was everything? Need anything to go? Pie maybe?" She asked offering a kind smile when Claire sat her empty mug down.

Claire returned her smile. "No thank you. Great coffee. I love your atmosphere."

"Are you new to Austin, or just visiting?"

Claire paused for a moment, then answered, "For now, I'm just visiting a friend; checking the city out."

Rae questioned further, "Oh? You staying downtown?"

She freely gave the info, "Yes. The Kimpton."

Rae took the opportunity to catch her again, since Seth hadn't arrived. "You should come back tonight. We will have a live band, decaf and fresh pies. I make them myself. Starts around eight."

Claire seemed a little hesitant, "Well, I may see you later then, thank you." And with that she walked out and jumped into a cab.

Seth walked in only five minutes after she had gone. Rae motioned for him to come back to the counter. He sat on his stool, and she began spouting off everything she had found out. "Claire is indeed here. She's quote 'visiting a friend'. She's staying at The Kimpton. Oh, and I invited her to come to Music and Brew tonight."

Seth was trying to process it all, searching her face for an explanation.

Rae reached out and grabbed his warm hand. "Claire was here. Here in my shop. She didn't know who I was, I'm sure of that. She sat on the couch and had coffee. I can tell she's a knockout when she actually consumes calories. Seth, my heart went out to her. She's obviously struggling. I don't know. I guess I'm putting myself in her shoes. She was with you for a long time. You and I have been close for a short time, and if you told me you were leaving, I'm not sure how I would react either."

Rae was surprised to see Seth's eyes get a little misty.

He said quietly, "Rae, your heart went out to her because you are an angel. You love people. I do too, and I hate being the cause of someone's pain. The last couple of years we were together things began to change. It was just comfortable, but there was no real passion. Hell, we never had much chemistry. She was Jenny's friend first, and we were kind of pushed together by our families. The words I grew to hate the most were 'You look like the perfect couple'. That's not what will carry you through life with someone. She's in love with the idea of us, the image of us. I can't live like that. I need to be with someone I can't live without."

Rae finally took a breath. She had so many thoughts running through her head.

Seth continued, "I'm not sure how to proceed. Do I go to The Kimpton and wait for her? Do we just wait to see if she comes back here tonight?"

Rae thought for a moment, "I don't think we should seek her out. She came here without you knowing. As far as she knows, you have no idea."

He nodded in agreement and added, "Okay, so we wait and see." He finally smiled. "Thank you, Rae. For…you." He pulled her across the counter and put his lips on hers. It was sweet and brief. It was like a promise. A promise that no matter what, they were not going to let each other down.

Seth returned to his office. Between baking, Rae started a list of things she would need for Thanksgiving. It was less than two weeks away. Up until two years ago, she had always spent the holidays with her grandmother. After she passed, Rae spent them alone. This would be the first time in her life she planned for a large family gathering. It was a little stressful, but she was beyond excited.

Seth had been back working for a couple of hours when he got a text from Claire.

Hey you! I'm in Austin! Wanted to surprise you. Can you meet me at The Big Brew coffee shop at 8?

Seth sighed at the nonchalant tone of her text, replying only with: **Sure.**

When Seth walked in at seven thirty, Sarah pointed back towards the steps. Rae had gone to freshen up after working all day. He knocked on her door. Rae opened it and dragged him inside. She threw her arms around his neck and covered his mouth with hers. He held on tight and responded with enthusiasm. They were still clinging to one another when the kiss ended.

"Happy to see me?" he asked.

Rae purred, "Mmmmm. I don't want you to change your mind."

He moaned. "Never." He wanted to throw her down on the bed and show her just how much he wanted to be with her, and her only, but the sounds of the band warming up signaled it was time to go back down.

When they reached the bottom of the steps, Sarah handed Rae a pie server. It was quite busy already. Rae went into the kitchen to get to work. Seth sat at the counter on his normal stool beside the cash register, and Quincy brought him a full mug of decaf.

Claire was prompt, walking in at eight on-the-dot. She sat beside Seth with a smile on her face. Quincy was happy to see her and ran over to take her order.

When he stepped away, Seth spoke, "So, what brings you here? I'm definitely surprised."

Claire touched his arm. "Seth, I was desperate. I have been tormented ever since we broke up. Then, you had to come back home looking wonderful. I wanted you to look terrible. I wanted you to be as unhappy as I was, but you were content. I never expected you to fall in love with Austin so quickly. I had to come see for myself why you seem fine, why you don't miss me at all. Jenny told me you've met someone, but really Seth, so soon? You can't possibly be serious about her."

Her words stung, but he smiled and said, "Actually, I am serious about Rae, but I was happy here before I met her. My job is great. The city is amazing, and then I saw Rae. She didn't know who I was, but she'd already stolen my heart. I never felt that way with us. I want you to find it too one day, Claire."

A tear rolled down her cheek. "Seth…I'm sorry. I had no idea. I don't know what I'm doing here. I've never seen your eyes light up this way. I'm so embarrassed."

She stood to leave. Seth stopped her. "No, Claire. Don't go. Sit. Drink your coffee. Enjoy the music. We can sit here together, right?"

She sat back down. "Okay…Yes, we can."

Rae walked out to serve some customers sitting beside the stage. Claire noticed the way Seth watched her.

She looked at Seth and asked, "That's Rae, isn't it?"

He smiled and looked down at his coffee mug. "Yes, that's Rae." He was blushing. At that moment, Seth could see that Claire felt some closure.

Rae walked by to go back to the kitchen, but didn't pay attention to them when she passed. She wanted to give them time and didn't want to overwhelm Claire.

Claire's phone rang, "It's Jenny," she told him as she answered it. "Jenny, hey. Yes, I'm fine. I'm sitting here with Seth now. Yes, he is fine, too. Jenny, I'm such a fool. He's not mine anymore. Austin is perfect for him, and I'm pretty sure he's in love. Yeah, it's quite obvious. I promise I'll call you in the morning."

Claire put her hand on Seth's arm, "You are, you know. In love. Head over heels."

He nodded in agreement, "I think you may be right. I want you to meet her, but you don't have to if you don't want to."

She squeezed his hand. "It's okay. I'd like to see her again. We met earlier today. She's the one who invited me to come here tonight. I hope I don't make her uncomfortable. I've seriously never been more embarrassed."

He shook his head. "No. She's the most understanding person I know. I'm going to get her. I'm sure she's in the kitchen."

Seth was all smiles when he walked in. Rae melted when he grabbed her waist and looked down into her eyes with his perfect white teeth gleaming.

"I take it, it's going well?" she asked.

He answered her with another seductive kiss.

Rae caressed his face. "Thanks for that. Can I come see her? She didn't leave, did she?" She slid from his grasp, and handed him two plates with warm caramel pie.

When he sat it in front of Claire, she said, "Oh my goodness. I haven't had caramel pie in ages."

"It's the easiest to make," Rae said. "I'm so glad you came back! I hear you've known this guy for a long time."

Claire took a bite, and answered with a full mouth, "Yep. We were quite the pair for a while. I'm happy to see how happy Seth is, and to meet you."

Rae gave her a genuine smile, "Thank you. I'm pretty fond of him."

Seth grabbed Rae's hand. They talked about the company Seth worked for and about The Big Brew.

After she'd finished her coffee and pie, Claire sighed. "Phew. The pie was wonderful. I think it's about time for me to head back to the hotel. I'm leaving early in the morning." She dialed her cell for a cab.

"Yeah, I gotta clean up," Rae said. "Please come back sometime."

Claire gave her a hug and said, "I will. You have the best place here."

Seth stood and said, "Let me walk you out."

He leaned over and whispered into Rae's ear, "I want you to know you are the best. I'm so glad I saw you through the bookstore window.

Can I stay here tonight, angel?" He nuzzled her ear. His deep, sultry voice alone had her humming yes.

The cab was already pulling up in front of the door. Claire patted Seth's arm, "Sorry, I've been so crazy lately. You two belong together. Your family is going to love her. I'm really happy for you." She squeezed his arm and got into the cab. He watched it drive away.

A weight had been lifted off his shoulders, and he had never been more sure about his feelings for Rae. While he was still standing outside, he got a call from Jenny.

"Hey Sis. Yes, Claire just left to go back to her hotel. I couldn't have asked it to go any better. She's going home tomorrow. Hey Jen…tell mom I'm going to need her to bring something to Austin for me. Yep, I've never been more sure of anything in my life."

After shoving his phone back into his pocket, Seth stood on the sidewalk and looked around. It seemed crazy, but he had already made so many memories right here between The Book Bank and The Big Brew. Good and bad, there was nowhere else he would rather be.

He turned to see Rae leaning against the open door to her shop, observing him with loving eyes. She never failed to mesmerize him. When he grinned, she stepped out to join him and he wrapped her up close in his arms.

They began to hear knocks on the big shop window. Her customers were peering out, all of them giving thumbs up. Seth and Rae started giggling. He threw her back into a dip and planted the most romantic kiss on her lips. They walked back inside, and everyone clapped and cheered. Seth gave the guys high fives.

Rae calmed the crowd. "Okay. Okay. Enough everyone! Let's get back to eating pie."

Seth exclaimed, "A slice for each of you. It's on me!"

The crowd cheered again.

"Well, that should take care of every pie in the kitchen," said Rae. She was technically off, but they were having so much fun, they stayed to help Sarah and Quincy until the last customer had gone.

It was eleven-thirty, and the shop was empty and quiet. Rae went up front to cut out the lights, and make sure the door was secure. She flipped the switch, and Seth looked up at her. His tall form was outlined by the light from the steps where he stood. She patted the green velvet couch, motioning for him to sit. He made his way to her, as she sat at one end.

"Come here. Lay your head in my lap."

He stretched his long body out on the couch, and they watched the still city through the window. She played with his thick brown hair, and he squeezed her knee. A few couples walked by hand in hand. An older gentleman went by walking his dog. Rae tugged up the bottom of his shirt and started to scratch his back. He groaned, closing his eyes.

"I've never had this before," Seth said. "Just being. Simply being here together, not really doing anything. It feels amazing."

He rolled onto his back to look up at her in the dim light.

Rae smiled at him. "I just want you to relax. I don't want you to have to think about anything. Like you said, just be."

He took hold of the hand that wasn't playing with his hair and said, "As long as it's being with you, I'm happy." His eyes were glowing with contentment. "Can we make a pact?"

She smiled and nodded yes.

"Let's always remember this feeling. This feeling that we're here for each other; that we want to take care of each other. Later, if we have a fight, or go through a hard time, let's never forget."

Rae's eyes were serious. She had never had this before either. She realized she could never lose this man. Seeing the look on her face, Seth stood up, and pulled her to him. She clung to him and buried her face in his chest, pleading, "Just don't ever let me go."

He tightened his embrace. "Never. I promise."

They went upstairs and spent the night side by side in a deep slumber.

Chapter Nine

The following days went by in a whirlwind. Rae was pretty sure she had everything she needed for Thanksgiving. She and Sarah had already put up a Christmas tree and decorations to make the shop look more festive.

When Rae's cell beeped, she expected Seth, but the name Erik Noble displayed on the screen. She had forgotten all about Erik. Back in the Spring, she checked an item off of her bucket list. She had posed for Erik, a former college classmate. He immortalized her in a gorgeous oil painting. Erik was not interested in women, but he was the first man to make Rae feel sexy and comfortable in her own skin.

He had positioned her lying on her left side, on a milky, linen covered bed. A crisp white sheet was strategically placed across her hips, and an ample display of cleavage was visible. Her left arm extended over the edge of the duvet, her cheek rested on her bicep. Rae's long fingers almost touched the windowsill; teasing the rays of sunlight that shone through. Her green eyes were half closed, and her peach lips parted.

She hadn't mentioned it to Seth, because she honestly hadn't thought about it again, but now she received the text to let her know his art was now on exhibit, and her piece was featured.

She replied, letting him know she would be there. She called Seth and asked him to meet her at the gallery the next night to check out her friend's show. He sounded a little jealous when she mentioned the artist was a friend, but she didn't tell him there was no cause for concern. She figured a little healthy competition would be fun, and he would quickly realize there was nothing to worry about with Erik.

Seth arrived first, and Erik noticed him as soon as he walked through the door. He was very attracted to Seth and watched for a few moments before introducing himself.

As a photographer, Seth appreciated most any kind of art. He paused to read the easel about the artist and his work. The front row of paintings displayed lovely subject matter. A field of bright blue flowers that seemed to sway in the wind. A glassy puddle of rain water, glistening on dark pavement. Seth could imagine the smell of a recent city rain.

Erik matched him in height. He was lean with dark eyes and jet-black hair. He began to glide over to Seth when Rae walked in. She hadn't seen Erik in ages and hugged him tightly. Seth was paying attention, but did not move to join them. She felt eyes on her and looked past Erik. She saw her heart standing there, watching her, and immediately felt bad that she played along with his jealousy. Seth was the best-looking creation in the room. She couldn't wait to peel that black tee over his head in the near future.

Erik disappointedly took note of their connection when he saw the fire in her eyes. Rae pulled him over to make introductions. Seth assessed her figure in maroon velvet dress pants, and lavender silk blouse as they walked over to him. She slid her arm around his waist, feeling the columns of taught muscle in his back. Her touch eased his mind. He secured her in place with his long arm, anchoring her to his side.

Both men were cordial with one another. Seth genuinely complimented Erik's talent. Rae was staring up at Seth as he spoke, and Erik soon excused himself with a wink in her direction.

Seth looked down, deep into her gaze, and whispered into her ear, "How am I supposed to enjoy the artwork when all I can look at is you?"

Rae felt her face flush, and her body vibrated with electricity. She leaned up nose to nose, and said, "I have something to show you."

She laced her fingers through his and pulled him past two more rows of paintings. There on the back wall hung a life size siren in oils. His angel. Erik had captured every perfect detail. Her hand looked realistic. The warmth of the sun seemed to radiate from the canvas. The look in her eyes enticing. Seth was speechless as he took it all in. He looked back at Rae who was watching for his reaction.

She whispered, "I love it so much." She was glowing even more than the work of art.

Seth said, "I have to have it."

Rae nestled against his side. "Seth, you don't have to do that."

He gave a short laugh, "Um, yes. I have to. I want it. Besides, I don't want it hanging in someone else's house. This belongs in my bedroom." She buried her head in his shoulder, a little embarrassed. "I'll make arrangements with Erik to pick it up at the close of the show." He spoke into her hair. "It's perfect. You're perfect."

They meandered through the rest of the rows, meeting up with Erik back at the front. He and Seth exchanged information and agreed to decide on a price later. They went their separate ways, so that Rae could finish her usual Sunday night ritual doing laundry.

The following day was filled with last minute preparations for her out of town guests. Seth's family would be arriving the next afternoon. The shop had been slow, so she was able to get a lot done. Rae finished her shift, had a long shower, and sat still naked on her bed. She scrolled through her phone, feeling a deep pull to see Seth.

It was seven, and he'd probably just be getting in from a run.

She sent him a text.

Can I come to your place for a little while?

He responded quickly.

Just thinking the same thing. Give me twenty minutes and bring your toothbrush. I want you in my bed tonight.

His words made her whole body shiver with anticipation. She didn't bother with underwear, just pulled on grey yoga pants and her most worn out Longhorn sweatshirt. She threw her hair into a bun and grabbed her necessities.

Rae didn't knock. She let herself in and saw him outside, standing against the rail in his grey sweats, looking ripe for the picking. His dark hair was still wet from a shower, and that lit the fire inside her. She poured herself a glass of wine, swallowed it down hastily, and proceeded to sneak up behind him.

Seth had no idea she was so close and yelped when she slapped him on the butt. He spun around wide eyed. Rae couldn't contain her laughter.

"Hey now! It's your turn next," he warned in a deep, playful tone. He began to laugh, and Rae jumped back inside, and leapt up onto the sofa. He stalked around her, his eyes gleaming. When he came around, his long arm easily reached her, and he gave her a forceful swat in return. She yelped herself. It had a real sting to it. The laughing had ceased.

Rae slid over the back of the couch and dashed to the kitchen. Seth chased her around the island and caught her from behind as she tried to make a move towards the bedroom. His hands were on both of her arms. He held her tight, his tall body pressed against hers. She felt his erection.

"Now, now. Are you being a bad girl? Do you need another spanking?" He spoke like a teacher scolding his student. Rae wanted to be bad. Her reply shocked her own ears when it came out of her mouth.

"I want you to fuck me." She was glad he couldn't see her face, because she grimaced a little when she said it, but she meant it. She was burning for Seth to be forceful with her; to take control. He was surprised by her words but had never felt so masculine. He also knew she felt safe enough with him to play this dominating game.

He had not taken this role before, but had fantasized about it. He lowered his voice to a darker tone, "Stay right where you are. Don't move." He closed the drapes covering the large balcony windows. He turned out all the lights except for one lamp by the front door.

Rae was shivering with excitement, as she watched the most gorgeous man she had ever seen move around the room, preparing to master her.

Seth completely undressed, and again stood up against her back, pulling the back of her shirt up far enough to place himself against her. His naked masculinity seared the flesh above her buttocks like a hot iron. He was more than ready for her. He breathed in the floral scent of her hair. He pulled it down, and tugged lightly, raising her face toward the ceiling. He bent down, kissed her neck behind her left ear, and nibbled her earlobe. Seth's wet tongue sampling her flavors instantly made her wet as well.

When she gasped, he let go of her hair. "Raise your arms," he growled. She obeyed. He slid the sweatshirt over her head and tossed it onto the island. He stayed right behind her. He placed her hands around the back of his neck and slid his large hands down her arms to find her breasts. She responded by arching her bottom against him and running her fingers through his hair. She tried her best not to make a noise. He slid his hands down further to grip her waist hard with his long fingers and rubbed himself against the small of her back. She let go of his neck and grabbed his hands. He pulled her left arm behind her back, and swatted her right buttock saying, "Did I tell you to let go?" She shook her head no.

He kept hold of her arm, and bent down to slide her yoga pants off, revealing her bare bottom. "Oh, you have been a bad girl," he said with hot breath, kissing the sensitive skin. His sense of carnality was taking over. Even though he was intimately close to her most private places, Rae felt exalted. He was reveling in her being like a tasty treat. He remained on his knees, and ordered her to turn around. He kissed her navel, then licked lower, as his hands delighted her from behind. Rae grasped his dark, damp hair. He threw her right leg over his shoulder, and found her sweetest spot. The pleasure he was giving her was almost unbearable. She felt like she was losing her mind. Her knees almost buckled, and he swiftly picked her up and sat her down on the back of the couch. When his mouth returned to finish her undoing, she couldn't help but to utter sounds of indulgence. Her body shuddered as she relished in complete ecstasy.

She whispered shyly, "Oh, Seth please…fuck me." His eyes were so dark. He stood, and maneuvered her body to bend over the sofa, and instructed her to stay put. Seth was gone for only a few seconds as he retrieved a condom from his bedroom. He slid it on, taking in the view. He slowly entered her from behind, then began to take her deeper, over and over, pounding her hard against the leather. They were both groaning louder and louder as they unleashed cries of euphoria when Seth spent what energy he had left in release.

Rae laid, draped over the sofa whimpering with satisfaction. Seth leaned down to whisper in her ear, "Rae, you're exquisite." His hands were still all over her body. He couldn't get enough. She raised up and turned to face him. He had a very satisfied look on his face, and she never felt more confident.

She continued to play with him, "Did I please you?"

He smiled a naughty grin and replied, "Oh yes. I've never wanting anything more than I want you. I have to have you."

She kissed his forehead, his chin, his jaw and whispered, "I'm yours. Always." Her tongue found his. He carried her to his bed, and sweetly possessed her again.

Chapter Ten

The Reagans made a stop at their hotel to drop off luggage, then went to Seth's place. They all piled into his apartment. His mother, Eve, gave him a long hug, and her heard her sniffling. He pulled back to look at her face. She was crying and smiling at the same time. She said, "I've got something for you dear." She took a red velvet box from her coat pocket and placed it in his hand. He embraced her again, "Thanks Mom." Jenny's kids were already hanging from the balcony rail, and Clay's son was jumping on the couch. He was thankful Rae had offered her place for the holiday meal.

Sarah and Quincy were covering the rest of the week before the holidays, so that Rae could spend time with the family. Before meeting up with them at Seth's apartment, she baked enough pie to supply the days she would be off.

Rae rode the escalator up to the fifth floor. She stood in front of Seth's door, pausing for a moment. She could hear children laughing on the other side. She straightened the collar of her denim button down shirt and tightened her ponytail. She was feeling her nerves as she knocked once on the door. Before she could knock a second time, a large, gloved hand grabbed her wrist, and jerked her backwards. Much to her horror, it was Sam Preston.

He had her wrist with one hand. The other was in his coat pocket, where she assumed he was holding a gun. He snarled between his teeth, "Don't make a peep. Get back into the elevator."

Rae was terrified and forgot how to breathe. She wasn't even sure if anyone heard her one and only knock. She pleaded to the universe that they did.

Seth had heard the knock. He opened the door with a smile, only to see the elevator door closing with Sam and Rae inside. Seth shouted, "Clay to call 911!" and bolted down the stairway. He had no gun, so he was unsure what he was going to do, but he knew he couldn't let Rae be taken from the building.

Rae knew the same, that her odds weren't good if Sam got her to his car. When they stepped into the lobby, she tried to stall him, urgently pleading, "Sam wait! Wait! Sam! Seth and I broke up."

The false information had him interested enough to slow down his pace, but he was still dragging her.

He growled, "Then what are you doing here?"

She stopped walking, and did her best acting job. "I came to get my things from his apartment."

His eyes narrowed, and she could tell he wasn't sure if she was being truthful. He asked, "Why are all the others here?"

She quickly fabricated a lie. "He's going back to Utah. They came to help him move his things before the holidays."

Seth had stayed behind the door to the stairs, watching through the small window. He saw that Rae had Sam halted, and was trying to bide her time as long as she could. Clay had followed him down to see if he needed some help. Knowing the police were on their way, they decided to take action if Sam got her anywhere near the front door.

When Seth's neighbor Lucy walked in, Rae panicked. She pulled Sam's mouth down to hers to distract him. She bravely kissed him until she heard the elevator bell signal its upward climb. Sam tasted like stale liquor, and her stomach lurched with the need to vomit. She suppressed the urge, and Sam had let go of the gun in his pocket to put his arms around Rae. She had successfully turned his back to the front door, as well, so that he didn't see the blue lights of the cop cars as they pulled up. She grabbed both his wrists as hard as she could, the gun residing safely in the coat pocket, when the police came through the doors with guns drawn.

"Sam! Don't make a move," they shouted. He wrestled to free himself from her grip, as two cops tackled him.

Seth and Clay burst out into the lobby and ran to Rae. As Seth scooped her up, tears rolled down his face. Clay patted his back to reassure him the terror was over.

Rae wiped his cheeks and said, "Seth. I'm here. I'm fine. I love you, Seth."

He buried his nose in her neck, "I love you. I love you so much, Rae. When I watched that elevator door close, I…I didn't know…I didn't know if…" He couldn't continue. He dared not dwell on thoughts of what could have happened. He let her down, and she wrapped herself around his waist, as they watched Sam being put into the police cruiser.

It dawned on her that the rest of the family was upstairs. "Oh my gosh, Seth! I've ruined everything. What are we going to tell your family? Oh, sorry. I was almost kidnapped by a stalker, and—"

"Rae. My family is fine. We will tell them everything, and boy, do we have a story to tell."

Chapter Eleven

To make things simple, Seth ordered pizza, and everyone spread out on every surface of his apartment. He and Rae began to tell the almost unbelievable tale of how they met.

Seth began, "So, I had settled in here and been working a few weeks. I hadn't explored the city all that much, and went to The Book Bank to see what kind of photography books were hot sellers in Austin." He paused, placing his hand on Rae's knee, and continued, "There she was."

The family gave a collective "Aww."

"Rae and her art book. She didn't notice me staring at all. It was like…" He looked into her eyes, "Love at first sight."

Rae gave him a short, sweet kiss.

"Seth hasn't told you what happened that day. How brave he was. Well, I stood by the front window and felt eyes on me, and this tall, handsome man was looking at me. I mean, at first, I thought he was surely looking at someone else. This perfect face." Her hand went to his cheek. "But…there on the sidewalk, a horrible man had a gun! He mugged a poor old woman, and she was trying to give him her ring, but it fell, and he cocked the gun. I watched Seth put himself in the way. I heard the gunshot. I saw it all in disbelief, and I called 911. The people outside were in shock. I mean, things like this don't happen here. I ran out and put my scarf to his side. He was bleeding."

The family gasped, "Honey! Why have we not heard of this before now," Mom scolded.

"Oh Mom, I know I should have told you. When I woke up in the hospital and knew it wasn't too serious, I just didn't want to worry you all. I guess I'm a lot like someone else we know," he said looking at Dad.

Clay chimed in, "He has a point."

"Okay, I have to know what happened next," Jenny added.

"What'd it feel like to get shot," asked Jenny's youngest Matthew.

"Terrible! Felt like horse kicked me in the side, and I couldn't hear very well, because it happened so close to my ear. I think I just went down to the ground."

"Yes, you did. The ambulance took him away, I told the cops what happened, and had to just go back to work, wondering if he made it or not."

Jenny shook her head, "I can't even imagine." Her husband Drew hooked his arm around her, pulling her close.

Seth continued, "I was so lucky. The bullet went clean through, only hitting my lung. It missed anything that would have caused major bleeding. I just had a chest tube overnight, and I was back home in two days. The next three nights I had vivid dreams about it. I kept seeing Rae's face through the window. I just knew I had to find you," he said softly turning to her.

"And you did." She looked back at the enamored faces. "I lured him into my shop with the promise of free coffee," she laughed sweetly.

"Oh, you lured me in, huh?" He leaned in and kissed her neck.

"Okay. Enough kissing," little Matthew whined.

Everyone laughed.

"Oh, you all will love The Big Brew. It will be perfect for Thanksgiving," Seth gushed. "We will see it tomorrow and grab lunch there."

Seth pulled Rae up from the floor where she had been sitting and placed another sweet kiss on her lips. The way they looked at each other affirmed to the others of their deep mutual affection. Mom thanked Rae for helping to save her son's life, even though he'd been a stranger to her then.

Rae had never experienced this kind of love before. She couldn't count on one hand the number of people she truly called family. Seth sat on the couch and drew her down to sit in his lap. He held her tightly, nuzzling her neck with his nose.

The kids were looking sleepy. The family gathered up to go back to the hotel.

When the room was quiet again, Rae turned into Seth's chest, and cuddled up to his warmth and security. She marveled, "I love your family so much, and I love you more."

He kissed the top of her head, "I'm positive they already adore you, angel. I don't what I would have done if things didn't turn out the way they did today."

Rae put her hand on his beating heart. "It's obvious the universe is on our side, and your family didn't get hurt. That's the most important thing to me."

Chapter 12

Rae stayed the night, but had to get back to her place early the next morning to take care of a few things before Seth and the rest of the family arrived. She showered, checked her Thanksgiving list again, and headed to the kitchen to plan the lunch menu. She had taken pride in the successful business she had built, and was happy, but Rae had never been happier around this time of year. The past couple of years, she hadn't cared or payed much attention. She thanked her lucky stars that she had found Seth. He was a treasure that could never be replaced.

She and Quincy pushed some tables together to accommodate the large Reagan family for lunch. Sarah straightened pillows on the sofa when she announced, "Rae, your special guests are here."

Rae smiled as she watched the group walk up, children skipping along, tugging on their parents. Clay had Seth's camera in hand, but there was no Seth. Just then, she heard the rumble of his motorcycle. The group gathered around the front window, waiting for him. Rae waved to them, and the children waved back. Seth took his time, pulling a small red box from the pocket of his black leather jacket. He stopped in front of the large shop window and lowered himself onto one knee. Rae's heart skipped a beat then stopped.

She slowly walked closer to the glass to wrap her brain around what was happening, and to make sure it was real. As Seth gazed up at her, she watched as his family clasped each other's hands. He opened the box, smiling brightly. Then winked and mouthed the words, "Come here."

Rae gasped, and rushed out to seize him, almost knocking him over.

Clay snapped pics, and a crowd that had gathered on the sidewalk began clapping. The Book Bank employees had also joined in on the spectacle.

Seth's father, Maxwell, chuckled, "Is that a yes?"

Rae pulled away to let Seth breathe. They stared into each other's green eyes. Seth simply said, "Marry me, my love."

"Yes!" She answered hastily and her lips found his.

Acknowledgements

The biggest thanks to my loving husband, Brian, for his never-ending support. Much love and gratitude to Sophia Henry who gave her time, expertise and advice which made my first writing endeavor possible.

GINGER LEE, a life long Tennessee native, spent many years working as a surgical scrub technologist and surgical first assistant. She began writing at the age of thirty-six and spends her days raising her daughter, traveling with her husband and attending concerts with friends.

gleewrites.com

@gleewrites

Made in the USA
Columbia, SC
18 June 2022